HER DESERT FAMILY

BY

BARBARA McMAHON

MILLS & BOON®

First published in Great Britain 2004
Large Print edition 2005
Harlequin Mills & Boon Limited,
Eton House, 18-24 Paradise Road,
Richmond, Surrey TW9 1SR

© Barbara McMahon 2004

ISBN 0 263 18552 4

Set in Times Roman 17 on 18½ pt.
16-0505-42985

Printed and bound in Great Britain
by Antony Rowe Ltd, Chippenham, Wiltshire

CHAPTER ONE

THE sun shone through the old stained-glass windows casting a rainbow of hues on the polished casket. Bridget Rossi stared at the colors, numb to all feelings. It still hadn't sunk in that her beloved papa was forever gone. At his insistence, she'd brought him home to Italy. This old church was far grander than the one they'd attended in San Francisco. Today it was filled with relatives she hardly knew. And strangers who had known her father as a young man before he'd emigrated to America.

Aunt Donatella sat beside her in the first pew. On the other side of her, Bridget's brother Antonio sat, quiet and solemn. Probably wondering how long before he could return to the States and get back to business.

Behind them, Bridget heard the hushed murmurs as people waited for the start of the service. How slowly the minutes passed.

The sound level rose, changed in pitch. Curious, Bridget turned to look at the back of the church. Francesca always made an entrance, she thought fondly as she saw her older cousin enter the sanctuary with a flourish. One by one everyone in the place turned to stare. Francesca loved it, Bridget knew. Tossing back her dark wavy hair, she sauntered down the center aisle as if she were on a catwalk, modeling the latest in Italian fashion. The chic black dress looked terrific on her. Her style and flare made everyone else look dowdy.

Bridget glanced at her own black suit. It was subdued and somber. With an inward sigh, she scooted closer to Aunt Donatella to make room for her cousin. She would never have the panache Francesca had if she lived to be a hundred.

Francesca and the stranger who accompanied her came straight to the front pew. She waved at family members, blew a kiss at another cousin, turning to murmur something to the tall man standing beside her.

Bridget hadn't met this one yet. Francesca played the field, bringing a new escort to every event she attended. Still, it seemed odd to bring a casual friend to a family funeral.

"Hello, Bridget," Francesca said when she leaned over to hug her, kissing the air near her cheek. The perfume she wore threatened to choke Bridget, but that was Francesca—over the top on most things.

"I'm so glad you could make it," Bridget whispered, clinging for a moment. Francesca was the only relative she felt comfortable with in Italy.

"Of course I made it. He was my uncle. I loved him, too." Francesca greeted her mother and Antonio, then settled in the pew beside Bridget and turned to the man who sat beside her. "Rashid, this is my cousin from America, Bridget Rossi. Bridget, this is His Excellency, Sheikh Rashid al Halzid.

He leaned forward a bit and offered his hand. Bridget took it, surprised by the gesture. Most of Francesca's men never took notice of anyone else—they only had eyes for Francesca.

When had her cousin started dating a sheikh? He was gorgeous, and so far removed from Bridget's world she was instantly fascinated. Trust her cosmopolitan cousin to captivate such a sexy man.

''My sincere sympathy on the loss of your father,'' he said in English with a charming trace of an accent which sounded British.

She nodded and withdrew her hand, reminded instantly of where they were and why. He settled back, looking as out of place in the church as she felt. Who was this man with his air of authority and what relationship did he have with her beautiful cousin?

Momentarily her grief had been forgotten as a spark of interest bloomed. She tried to remember if she'd heard Francesca was seeing anyone special, but between caring for her father and working, she'd not had time to keep in close contact with her over the last few months. No one had mentioned anything in the two days she'd been in Italy.

The priest entered and the service began.

It seemed like only seconds passed before they were heading for the cemetery—the final resting place for her papa, beside his beautiful, and beloved, Isabella.

When Bridget exited the church walking quietly beside her older brother, she was surprised to see a white limousine parked behind the one dark one the funeral home provided. She glanced around and saw Francesca clinging to Rashid's arm heading for the luxury vehicle. She had not had a chance to say more than a few words to her. She'd hoped they would ride to the cemetery together, but it looked as if Francesca had other ideas. Bridget would ride with her aunt and brother as originally planned.

''Perhaps your cousin would care to join us,'' Rashid suggested to Francesca, pausing to look over at Bridget. ''You two have not seen each other for a while, and I know this is a trying time.''

Francesca smiled, trailing one finger along his cheek. ''If she were not already going with her brother and my mother, that would be fine. But she'll have to go back with them as we'll be returning directly to the airport. Maybe it would be less confusing for her to stay with the original plans.''

''Perhaps you wish to ride with them. I know you haven't seen your mother in several months. We have time enough after the graveside service to return to the airport. And if not,'' Rashid said, ''we can always change our departure time. If you wish to visit with your relatives, please do.''

''That would be nice, Rashid,'' Francesca said.

Rashid believed in the importance of family and Francesca's young cousin looked pathetically lost at the moment. Donatella Bianchetti was speaking with friends who crowded around. The man who had been introduced as Antonio Rossi was paying no attention to his sister. She could use some comfort from Francesca.

He contrasted the two women as Francesca called to Bridget. Had he not known they were related, he would never have suspected. Francesca was tall and model thin. Her glossy dark hair was thick and wavy. Her eyes held mystery and a hint of recklessness that was appealing. They'd been friends for a number of years. He enjoyed her company for as long as she stayed around. But her lifestyle was more flighty than his. After a brief visit, she'd be on her way to another photo shoot, or a modeling venue.

Bridget Rossi, on the other hand, was what the Americans called wholesome. Her dark auburn hair seemed to catch fire in the sun. Her figure could not be described as thin, but it was definitely all woman. Her eyes were red-rimmed and sad from the service. She'd cried several times, as if the wrench of parting with her father was more than she could deal with. But her skin was translucent and delicately tinted, and she carried herself with quiet dignity.

Rashid caught himself. What was he doing, comparing the two women? He was Francesca's friend. There was nothing between them other than friendship. Bridget he'd just met. He knew nothing about her beyond she had just lost her father.

When Francesca asked her to join them on the ride to the cemetery, Bridget jumped at the chance. She loved being with her glamorous cousin. They spent too little time together. Bridget would be returning to America in a couple of days. Who knew how long before Francesca would visit? The ride would give them a chance to catch up.

Bridget understood a haute couture model was in high demand. Francesca had been a much sought after super model in Europe for as long as Bridget could remember. But she still wished her cousin would come back to the States with her for a few weeks. Just until she had gotten used to her papa being gone.

Bridget brushed her fingers beneath her eyes. She'd cried during the service and hoped the mascara she'd put on was as waterproof as claimed. It was bad enough to be the plain woman in the car without looking like a raccoon.

The ride to the old cemetery was short. Bridget sat between Francesca and Rashid listening as her cousin brought her up-to-date on all her activities. Sometimes Bridget knew Francesca elaborated on actual events. Still, her lifestyle was glamorous and exciting, compared to that of a librarian in San Francisco.

Conscious of Rashid beside her, however, she had difficulty concentrating on Francesca's tales. She should be focusing on what Francesca was saying, or on the coming graveside service, not be so consumed with awareness of the stranger beside her.

His aftershave lotion was spicy and reminded her of wide-open spaces. It was not sweet or cloying like some men wore. She looked at his hands resting on his leg-long fingers, neatly manicured nails. What did a sheikh do, she mused. Probably nothing which involved getting calluses on his palms or fingers. From what she'd seen, he was tall and slender, not an ounce of fat anywhere. She sighed softly. She had to watch everything she ate or she'd be as large as a house. Glancing at her cousin, she wished again she could be as slender as Francesca.

The car was far more luxurious than the one the funeral home had provided. Did Rashid live in Tuscany? Was that why he had a limousine handy? Not only did his clothing reflect his wealth, but his air of command, the arrogance that surrounded him, told the world he was a man to be reckoned with. He was used to getting his way instantly, she suspected. Of course, sheikhs probably had half a country at their beck and call. How had he and Francesca met?

"Have you and Francesca known each other for long?" she asked when Francesca made mention of Rashid accompanying her today to the funeral. Maybe small talk would help her deal with the rest of the day. He'd been kind enough to offer her a ride. He must expect some curiosity.

"We met a couple of years ago," he said.

"Do you live here in Italy?" His English was much better than her other cousins. And he had not tried to speak Italian with her, which was a definite plus in his favor. Her Italian was poor at best, and when surrounded by this branch of her family who spoke a hundred miles a minute, she felt lost and awkward. The patience her father had always shown was missing from her aunt and uncles. And her cousins ignored her, except for Francesca, or laughed at her attempts to speak Italian.

Not that she would be long in Italy. Once this sad task was accomplished, she would return home. To the loneliness that awaited with her papa no longer there.

Francesca laughed. "No. Contrary to what my family thinks, Tuscany is not the center of the universe. Rashid lives in Aboul Sari. He's the youngest son of the ruling sheikh,"

Francesca said. ''He kindly flew me here to-day to attend the funeral. I received the news at his home, where we were vacationing.''

''Oh, I didn't know. I thought you were at a shoot or something.'' Bridget looked at her. Francesca seemed relaxed, not annoyed to have her vacation interrupted. Of course her papa couldn't help dying while Francesca was on vacation, but would she have come if he had been buried in San Francisco, as Bridget had wanted?

''I'm taking a few weeks off from work. I can use the rest. Rashid has this fabulous home and some friends over from England. We've all been having a fabulous time.'' Did Francesca's tone convey more than a vacation?

Bridget felt like a fifth wheel. She should have ridden with Aunt Donatella and Antonio. She would definitely return with her aunt and let Francesca and her sheikh return to his wonderful home and not be jealous that she herself would be returning to her flat in

San Francisco, and taking up her life again without her beloved papa in it.

The simple service at the grave site was brief and moving. As she turned away for the last time, Bridget caught a glimpse of the tombstone for Isabella Rossi, her father's first wife and Antonio's mother. Her papa had his wish; he was buried by his precious Isabella. Not by Bridget's mother where Bridget thought he should have been. He and her mother had been married far longer than he'd been to Isabella. But he'd been so insistent at the end, she'd acquiesced.

Poor Mama, she thought. Even in death, Papa wasn't hers.

Bridget continued along the pathway, conscious of Rashid following closely.

Francesca had stopped to speak with one of their other cousins. She knew them all so well, having been brought up with them in the family enclave.

"What will you do now?" Rashid asked as Bridget stopped near the car that had brought her aunt.

"Return home. There is nothing for me here," she said gazing around at the peaceful cemetery. The old lichen-covered tombstones and monuments were so unlike the neat pristine headstones where her mother was buried. This cemetery was far older, and much farther from home.

"Yet you brought your father here."

"He insisted. He knew he was dying and made us promise to bring him back to the place he'd been born." She was trying to imprint the setting on her mind. She wouldn't be this way again any time soon. Another regret. She could have visited his grave as often as she did her mother's had he been buried in California.

"You would rather have buried him in San Francisco," Rashid stated quietly.

"My mother is buried there. She was his wife, too." Bridget couldn't keep the hurt from her voice.

He looked back at the grave site, read the stone beside the coffin.

"Isabella was his first wife?"

"Yes, she was Antonio's mother. Molly O'Brien was mine. Hired to take care of his baby son when his beautiful Isabella died. Later they married, and had me." Bridget had heard the story all her life. On the surface it sounded so romantic. But her papa had never loved her mother, and Mama had known it. How hard had that been? To live with a man who loved a woman long dead?

"Do you work in San Francisco?" Rashid asked, leaning against the limo, studying Bridget with dark eyes that seemed to see beyond what others saw.

She looked away, disturbed by the emotions he brought out in her. "I'm a librarian at a branch in the Sunset district. I have a small flat nearby."

"You did not live with your father, then."

She shook her head. "Maybe I should have. I wonder if I would have known he was sick before he admitted it. Maybe I could have done something."

"Most likely not."

She looked at him. "What would you know about it?"

"What do you think you could have done?"

"I don't know, taken him to the doctor sooner or something." She looked into his dark eyes again, and felt the world tilt slightly. Rashid's broad shoulders, dark hair and eyes, made a perfect foil for Francesca. Together they made a striking couple, both gorgeous and self-assured.

Had he and Francesca spent hours at the beach or beside a pool *vacationing* together? What else had they been doing that her summons interrupted?

For a moment, a pang of envy hit Bridget. She'd love to have some wonderful, sexy man sweep her away to some hidden hideaway and make wild passionate love day and night. She'd always thought she'd like to see the south seas. But a bower on the Mediterranean could be just as romantic.

"Has it been suggested that earlier care would have saved his life?" Rashid asked.

It took Bridget a moment to reply. The fantasy of sunbathing at the sea vanished. She shook her head. "No, but I still worry I should have done something."

"What does your brother think?"

"That nothing could have been done."

"Your father was older than most of a woman your age," he commented.

"He was over forty when Antonio was born. Even older when I came along. He immigrated to California as a young man, and had to make his way in the world before he could start his family. He built one of the finest restaurants in Little Italy, near Columbus Street. And another one near the Wharf. When he had money enough, he returned home to find a bride. His beautiful Isabella was fifteen years younger, but such a love they had."

Rashid's eyes held a hint of sardonic amusement. "Or so the story goes. You sound as if you've heard that before," he said.

She nodded. ''He spoke often of his beautiful Isabella—especially after my mother died. I guess he didn't think I'd mind, but I wish he'd loved my mother as much.''

Francesca looked up, spotting her with Rashid. She waved and began heading their way, only to be stopped by another small group of friends.

''I'm sure their marriage was satisfactory for both. Not everyone marries for love as you westerners think,'' Rashid said.

''You don't believe in marrying for love?'' Bridget knew she read too many romance novels, but to her the greatest bond in life was love. She had loved her father and mother. She adored her older brother and her cousin. Close friends also were loved. How much more love would she and her husband share, once she found the right man?

''There are many reasons for marriage. Love is fleeting. Or nonexistent. Strong foundations can be built on other grounds.''

''Like what?'' She couldn't believe she was debating love and marriage at the edge of a cemetery with this sheikh. She'd just met the man! She would probably never see him again after today—unless he and Francesca were serious about each other. Did Francesca know he held such cynical views of love?

"Arranged marriages have been the norm in my country for generations. Dynastic reasons are strong bonds. Merging families for financial reasons insures the continuation of many bloodlines."

Bridget looked at Francesca. Maybe she'd misread the situation. Maybe this was no different from any other fleeting relationship her cousin had had over the years. She couldn't imagine her settling for less than passionate, brilliant love.

"So you are not looking for marriage anytime soon?" Bridget said, trying to understand the relationship.

"I have been married."

She looked at him in surprise. "You have? What happened?"

"She died."

''Oh.'' Bridget didn't know what to say. He certainly didn't seem particularly sad about the fact. Yet she didn't know him at all, so how could she gauge his feelings?

''I'm sorry,'' she said.

''As was I. Fatima was a beautiful woman. Accomplished. And a delight to be with. I still miss her.''

She wasn't surprised to hear that. Rashid was extremely handsome and obviously liked to be with beautiful women. How sad he and his wife didn't get to share their lives together for more years than they had had.

''I'll get a ride back with Aunt Donatella. Francesca said you needed to get to the airport,'' Bridget said after a moment. The sooner she got away from Rashid, the better for her equilibrium. He was like a movie star, someone to dream about, but as far out of her experience as the landing on the moon. That hint of awareness that plagued her was probably due to heightened emotions because of the funeral. Tomorrow she'd laugh at the notion of being attracted to her cousin's friend.

She had to pack and get ready for her own flight home later tonight. She didn't need to know more about Rashid. If his and Francesca's friendship developed into something more, she'd learn about it in due time. And if not—

"You would be welcome to come stay with your cousin. I know you both grieve for the loss of your father. She spoke fondly of him on the ride here. Maybe a week or two in a new location would help ease the transition. Give you some breathing space before you return to life without your father in it," Rashid said.

She was struck by his insight. She had been dreading the return to San Francisco, to her flat only a few blocks from the home her father had lived in. There was so much to do with packing up his things, deciding whether to live in the family home or sell it. Her father had left it to her, and left the businesses to Antonio.

She had to learn to move on without her papa's comforting presence in the background.

Had Rashid felt the same kind of loss when his beautiful wife had died?

Bridget looked at her cousin. She'd love to spend a couple of weeks with Francesca. She couldn't remember the last time they'd spent more than two or three days together. Francesca rarely came to San Francisco. Her work was in Italy and other European countries; Bridget's was in California. The one time they'd tried to vacation together in Europe, Francesca had been offered a fabulous opportunity and took it to keep her name in the forefront of the fashion industry. Bridget had spent her week's vacation alone.

"I would not wish to impose," she said, yearning to accept.

"There are currently four other guests at the house, not counting my grandmother and my son who lives with me. One more would not be an imposition. Everyone will be visiting for another couple of weeks, so it may seem hectic. But come and spend time with your cousin." There was a hint of imperialistic command.

"You are very generous to a stranger you just met," she said, longing with everything in her to accept. But still she hesitated.

"Maybe I do it for Francesca. Don't you think she'd worry about you alone in San Francisco? How can she enjoy her visit if she has to fret about you?"

"I'm not exactly alone. I have my brother, my friends." But his explanation gave her a reason to accept. "Still, it would be wonderful not to return to San Francisco immediately."

"Come, visit me."

"Thank you. I would not wish to have my cousin fret." She wasn't sure, but she thought she saw sardonic amusement again in his eyes. But he looked away quickly, maybe she'd just imagined it.

A weight seemed to lift from Bridget's shoulders. She could postpone dealing with the reality of her father's death for a little while longer. Maybe it would be easier in a week or two. And she did have the time from her job.

"We will go with you while you pack," he said.

"Won't you miss your flight? I can make arrangements to follow later."

"I'm piloting the plane. We leave when I leave."

He snapped his fingers and a man standing beside his limousine hurried over. Rashid spoke to him rapidly in his language. When finished, the man bowed and hurried away.

Bridget listened bemused. She'd never known anyone who traveled by his own private plane, or piloted it himself. Or one who could summon anyone by a mere snap of the fingers. How cool. She had a feeling spending time with a sheikh would be unlike anything she'd ever experienced before. She'd have to make sure she took note of every delightful surprise so she could tell her friends when she returned home.

Francesca was enough of a star to give them endless hours of conversation whenever her friends asked Bridget what her cousin was doing. Now this. Who would ever believe plain Bridget Rossi was going to vacation at the palace of a sheikh?

Francesca bade farewell to the crowd surrounding her and sauntered down the path toward Rashid. Bridget watched her, wishing she had the knack to look so at ease in whatever circumstances she found herself. Wishing she could look sexy and sultry and fascinatingly interesting. Instead she was shy and self-conscious in unfamiliar settings and situations, though years of acting as her father's hostess had taught her ways to cover some of her uncertainty at social events. Even if she grew more confident as she aged, she'd never be as pretty as her cousin. Bridget had inherited her mother's Irish looks, dark auburn hair, fair skin with freckles scattered across her nose. Her blue eyes were boring, never as exotic as Francesca's.

"I'm sorry if I kept you waiting, darlings," her cousin said when she joined them. "Family duties, you know. I'm ready to leave now."

"I've invited your cousin to join us," he said smoothly.

"What?" Francesca looked at Bridget, then back to Rashid. "I'm surprised."

"I thought it would offer her time to come to terms with the change in her family. To give her a chance to spend time with her favorite cousin," he said. "Do you have a problem with my invitation?"

"Not at all. Thank you, Rashid. It's wonderful. We'll be able to talk all night and really visit. I'd never presume to invite her to your home, but since you were so thoughtful, I say terrific!" She gave him a quick kiss on the cheek.

"We'll run by your mother's so your cousin can pack and then we'll be off," he said.

Francesca glanced at her watch, "But our flight plan..."

"I've already changed it."

"I can always stay here," Bridget offered, uncertain once again about what she was doing.

"It would be my honor to have you visit my home," Rashid said gravely.

Bridget blinked. Put that way, how could she refuse?

The driver of the white limousine quickly whisked them to Aunt Donatella's home where Bridget made short work of packing. She had brought very little for her brief stay. Her aunt returned before she finished, so there was no wait to exchange farewells. Her aunt seemed to think time with Francesca would be just the thing for Bridget, though she was reluctant to have her leave.

"Come anytime," Donatella urged with one last hug. But Bridget wasn't sure she'd visit again. It was so different without her papa.

She'd never been close to the Italian side of her family except for Francesca. The few trips made over the years had primarily been to accompany her father on his visits to his brothers and sisters. Once Bridget left home for college at eighteen, she'd stopped making the annual trips to Italy.

She should have tried harder to connect. Her mother had been an orphan, so she had no family on that side. Aunt Donatella had been kind but she just didn't relate to her that well. Bridget sighed softly for what she couldn't change.

Everything moved swiftly until they were airborne. She had a seat near the back of the small jet, with an unobstructed view as they soared over the hills of Tuscany and the Italian coast before turning to head south.

Once over the deep blue Mediterranean Sea, Bridget grew restless staring at the endless expanse of water. She looked at the other occupants in the small jet. Rashid and Francesca were in the cockpit. Her cousin was laughing at something the man said, touching his arm flirtatiously. Bridget envied her cousin's ease in dealing with everyone, and wished she wasn't so shy, so uncertain.

The two solemn-faced men sitting across the aisle from her remained silent. Bodyguards, she suspected. Or servants of some kind. She hadn't forgotten how quickly one of them had responded to Rashid's summons.

Her gaze again moved to Rashid. She'd love to have an opportunity to sit in the front of the plane and watch as he piloted the craft. Anytime he wanted to go anywhere, he just filed a flight plan and took off as easily as she climbed into her car at home and drove away.

Was her cousin serious about this man? Francesca had never talked about getting married and having a family. Had that changed when she turned thirty? The work span of a model was limited. There were always younger women coming up through the ranks. Not that any of them were as beautiful as her cousin, Bridget thought loyally. But she wondered if Francesca worried about the future. Maybe she was planning to marry and leave her career at its peak.

She herself would like to find a man to love and marry. However, she did not plan to jump into anything just because her father had died and she felt more vulnerable than in the past. But she was already twenty-six, and not growing any younger.

Would she feel so vulnerable if she were Francesca? With such a fabulous career, she enjoyed everything—lovely designer clothes, an apartment in Rome and a flat on the Amalfi Coast. Hobnobbing with the jet set in Europe, and even a brief brush with fame in the United States. It would be hard to leave all that.

Bridget closed her eyes. She was tired, sad and feeling lost. Maybe she'd find renewed energy and determination visiting Rashid's country, she thought as she drifted off to sleep. Getting to know her cousin's friend should also prove interesting. And maybe dangerous to her equilibrium if that flare of awareness didn't dissipate by morning.

CHAPTER TWO

BRIDGET woke when the plane touched down. She felt too groggy and disoriented from so little sleep to be refreshed. When she checked her watch, she saw it was half past six. They would be eating dinner before too long. Then maybe she could escape to bed.

In the flurry of deplaning, and accounting for luggage and the carry-all her cousin had brought, Bridget soon found herself in a car with one of the bodyguards. Rashid had driven his two-seater sports car and her cousin rode beside him.

It seemed they roared along the highway at excessive speeds, but maybe she was imagining things. When they turned onto the private driveway, large wrought-iron gates barred the way. Rashid spoke into a small box and the gates swung wide. He zipped up the driveway, Bridget's car following more slowly. Bridget leaned forward to better see his home.

The asphalt wound around fountains, ponds and lovely old trees. She caught a glimpse of a building from time to time, but the landscaping was so lush and thick, she could only see a small segment at a time. Until they rounded the last curve and the villa stood before them.

Colorful blossoms of hibiscus and oleander crowded this part of the long driveway, providing a perfect frame for the wide veranda that encircled the bottom floor of the lovely structure. The white walls reflected the late-afternoon sun so brightly, Bridget fumbled for her dark glasses. The building looked almost too feminine for Rashid's strong masculinity, with the graceful lines and wide windows opened to the early-evening breeze.

She would have pictured him in glass and steel, or a high-rise soaring over the neighborhood.

The man sharing the back seat with Bridget opened the door and assisted her from the car.

Francesca was already heading for the opened front door, but Rashid remained beside the sports car, waiting for Bridget. He watched as she gazed around, her pleasure clearly evident. She studied each bank of flowers, raised her eyes to admire the old trees, and then the gentle sweep of walks that led to the center fountain.

"This is lovely," she said as she joined him.

He looked around absorbing what she saw instead of taking the gardens and grounds for granted. His staff had done an excellent job.

"I'm pleased you like it," he said formally. Looking at her, he gestured toward the house. "I told Francesca I'd see to getting you settled. You look tired. Would you care to skip dinner and go straight to bed?"

"Oh, no, thank you. I had a nice nap in the plane." She couldn't show up and immediately take to her room.

"We'll do a quick introduction to those who are around when we go inside and then I'll show you to your room so you can freshen up for dinner. We do not dress up unless it's a formal occasion.''

There were a couple of people about when they entered. Rashid introduced Bridget to Jack Dalton. Jack was a dedicated sportsman and long time polo player. He immediately tried to engage her in conversation about polo. Rashid could tell Bridget knew next to nothing about the sport as she nodded, trying to look interested. He rescued her from his friend's passion and found Marie Joulais nearby.

Marie greeted Bridget warmly when she was introduced and motioned at Jack, laughing. ''Stay out of his way tonight unless you want more of the same. Tomorrow is time enough for him to bore you to death about polo. He and Rashid are avid players. But he promised me a quick swim before dinner. I think we just have time.''

''Then we will see you at eight,'' Rashid said, grateful for her taking care of Jack. He enjoyed the man's company—they'd been friends from school days—but too much of

Jack at any one time could overwhelm anyone.

Rashid slipped his hand beneath Bridget's elbow and guided her toward the wide curving stairs that seemed almost suspended in midair. ''Come, I'll make sure you get to your room.''

An older woman, attired in black, stood near the stairs. She spoke to Rashid, then bowed and turned.

''My housekeeper, Marsella, would have shown you, but I will have the honor today,'' he said as explanation.

Normally he let his housekeeper see to his guests' needs. She'd been trained in his father's home and was excellent. But for some reason, he wanted to take Bridget up himself. She seemed lost and sad, which unexpectedly brought feelings of protection to the forefront.

Her arm was soft and warm. He didn't want to let go when they reached the stairs. The reluctance caught him by surprise. She was a guest in his house, no more.

He snapped orders to the man carrying Bridget's bag, and then to a maid standing near the top of the stairs. She scurried away down the wide hall. The sooner he had his guest safely ensconced in her room, the better. Perhaps he should have let Marsella take charge.

The room he escorted her to was done in pale yellow, the gauzy curtains at the windows billowing in the breeze. The rich carpet on the floor gave comfort to tired feet. The bed was huge, and high, with three steps on one side. Without them, he doubted she could reach the mattress without a running start.

Fatima had decorated their home. She'd had excellent taste and he had not found a need to change a thing since her death. Would Bridget like it?

"It's beautiful," she said as she surveyed the room.

"We gather in the solarium at eight for drinks. It's cutting it a little short I know, but we'll eat at eight-thirty and I think you could use some nourishment. It was a long and stressful day.'' He bowed slightly and left her alone in the lavish room.

His own quarters were in the opposite direction. As he headed there to freshen up, he wondered if Bridget would benefit from visiting, or whether it would prove too much on top of the strain of her father's illness and death. He hoped she would find comfort in Francesca's company. Maybe he could find some activities that would enable her to enjoy herself, while not being in the center of the hectic pace his other guests enjoyed.

Once again he found himself comparing the two cousins. Francesca was beautiful, polished. She conversed easily with statesmen and financiers. Bridget seemed shy and almost lost. He'd make it a point to spend some time with Bridget over the next few days to see if he could erase some of the sadness from her eyes.

Once the door closed behind Rashid, Bridget dismissed the maid and went to her suitcase where it had been placed on a rack and began to take the clothing out. She had not planned to stay anywhere but at her aunt's for a few days, so her variety of attire was limited.

She hung up the few dresses and pants she'd brought with her. Nothing she had was suitable for vacationing with a sheikh. Maybe she should return home.

Or ask for the nearest clothing store.

She smiled to herself. A much better suggestion. Would Francesca like to go shopping with her and suggest what she buy? With her cousin's flair for style, Bridget would come out way ahead.

She took a quick shower and donned a simple navy-blue dress. Brushing her hair back, she tied it with a matching bow. It was the best she could do—her eyes were still a little puffy from crying. She didn't like the sadness that seemed reflected there. Still, she wasn't out to impress anyone, just to recover a bit from her papa's death.

She started down the long hall wondering where the solarium was. If she'd been faster taking her shower, she might have met one of the other guests in the hall and could have gone with them. Or found Francesca. Now it was after eight. She was late, and lost.

She found the stairs easily. Bridget was surprised to see a small boy sitting on the top step, playing with a toy car.

"Hello," she said. Not that he would understand her, she didn't speak any Arabic.

"Hello." The boy responded and looked up at her. He said something rapidly which Bridget didn't understand.

"Sorry, do you speak English?"

"Yes. I speak French, too. *Parlez-vous Francais?*"

He didn't look old enough to speak three languages, she was impressed.

"No, I speak English and a bit of Italian." Bridget sat beside him on the top step. "I'm Bridget Rossi. I've come for a visit. Who are you?"

"I'm Mo. Mohammedan al Halzid. I live here."

"I think it was your father who invited me to visit."

"Is he home?"

The hopeful look in his eyes tugged at her heart. Bridget wanted to hug him tightly and send him off to find his father. But she didn't know where Rashid was at the moment. Most likely with the other guests in the solarium. Would this child know the way?

"He is home. I'm to join him and his other guests in the solarium. Do you know where it is? Maybe you can show me the way." Would Francesca come to look for her, wondering where she was? Or one of Rashid's servants?

He shook his head. "Little boys aren't allowed to bother his guests." He sighed a little and looked at his car.

"Maybe we can sneak down and find him without bothering the other guests," Bridget suggested. Her heart went out to the child. He looked so lonely. She knew how that felt. Surely his father didn't put guests before the well-being of his son?

For a moment Mo's eyes lit up. Then he shook his head. "I don't think I should."

"Well, I can tell your father you are hoping to see him before dinner. Would that work?"

He seemed to consider the situation before nodding gravely.

"How old are you?" she asked, captivated. What a darling child with his dark solemn eyes and long lashes. His black hair was short and shone beneath the light. Rashid was a lucky man.

"I'm five."

"Five and you already speak three languages? That's pretty impressive."

He nodded, looking proud.

"Good for you." Just then Bridget heard voices from the lower level. Rashid and one of his men walked into the foyer and headed toward the salon she'd seen earlier. He paused and looked up, surprised to see the two of them on the stairs. He said something to the other man and then climbed the stairs.

"What have we here?"

Mo launched into a rapid explanation in Arabic and launched himself at his father. For a split second, Bridget wished she could have done the same thing. The thought shocked her. Slowly she rose and smiled politely at the two. Rashid easily lifted the boy and held him in one arm, Mo flinging his arms around his father's neck.

"He wanted to see you before dinner," she said. "I wasn't sure of the way to the solarium, so I thought Mo could show me. But he said he wasn't allowed to bother the guests, so we were discussing the situation."

The two looked at her. Bridget saw the resemblance instantly. Even if she hadn't known Mo was Rashid's son, seeing them together would confirm it.

"You should be with Alaya," Rashid told Mo in English.

"I'm so impressed he speaks English," Bridget said.

"I have many friends who speak English, so better he learns it at an early age. He speaks French, as well. But he knows he's not to bother my guests."

"He wasn't bothering me. He just wanted to see you before he went to bed. It was nice to meet you, Mo. I expect I'll see you tomorrow?" Bridget said.

Rashid narrowed his eyes. "He usually doesn't associate with my visitors."

"Oh, sorry. I didn't realize that was off-limits."

"It's not. Usually the adults who visit don't come to spend time with a small child."

"I love children. I always wished I'd had lots of brothers and sisters. Antonio is several years older, and our interests don't mesh. Sometimes while growing up it felt as if I was an only child."

"I'm a only child," Mo said from his father's arms.

"And do you like that?" Bridget smiled at him.

"No, I want a brother. My dad has two brothers but I don't have any."

"Enough of that. Time for bed." Rashid and Mo started down the hall in the opposite direction from Bridget's room. He hesitated a moment when his son whispered in his ear. Then he turned. "Do you wish to see Mo's room?" he asked.

"I'd love to." She would be happy to see the little boy's room. It also would give her extra minutes before she had to face the room full of Rashid's guests. She hoped they all spoke English. As far as she knew, Francesca only spoke English and Italian. So if she fit in, Bridget would, too. At least in the language department. She wasn't so sure about the rest. She didn't normally number sheikhs among her acquaintances.

Mo's room was large, as were all the rooms in the villa. A nervous young woman quickly scolded Mo and apologized to Rashid. Bridget suspected it wasn't the first time the child had escaped her watch.

Rashid spoke quickly to her in obvious dismissal. She turned and left.

He set Mo on his feet. "Next time you run off without telling her, Alaya will get into trouble for letting you out of her sight. You don't want that, do you?'' Rashid said.

Mo shook his head. ''But I wanted to see you.''

''Show Miss Rossi your room and then you have to get ready for bed.''

Mo came and reached out his hand for Bridget's. She was charmed and clasped his small hand as he led her around the room pointing out toys, books, and games. Wistfully he looked back at his father. ''Do you play games?'' he asked Bridget.

''I do. Maybe you and I can play one tomorrow. Or I can read you a book. I see you have several in English,'' she said, spotting familiar covers.

He nodded, excitement gleaming. ''I like the English books. Tomorrow, promise?''

''Mo.'' Rashid said in a warning tone. He would not have his son badger a guest.

''If it's all right with your father, I would love to read to you. But I need to fit in with his plans first.'' She faced Rashid. ''It would be a pleasure.''

"You are here to rest after your loss, not baby-sit my son," he said stiffly. Truth to tell, not one of his guests even wished to see his son. Rashid was proud of Mo, but knew a child's place was not with adults.

Soon the boy would be old enough to attend boarding school. Rashid remembered leaving home at seven, and all the years in England and France he spent studying. He wanted to hold on to his son a little longer. Mo seemed much too young to be sent away in two years time.

"If I volunteer, it's okay. Shouldn't I be allowed to do what brings me happiness if I'm to get over Papa's death?" Bridget broke into his thoughts.

"And reading to a small boy you just met would do that?" Skepticism rang in his voice. Was she trying to impress him? he wondered cynically.

"I love assisting the children's librarian at work when she needs help at story book hour. Unless you don't wish for me to read to him?"

Rashid studied them both for a moment. "It would be unusual, but acceptable." What game was she playing? For a moment he wondered if she planned some sort of campaign to show him what a doting mother she could be to his small son. Only, she seemed much more interested in Mo than in him at the moment.

His father would say he had a swelled head, thinking women fawned over him. When they did, he knew it was for his position and wealth, more than anything else. He hoped Bridget wasn't one of those.

She smiled at Mo. "I'll come by in the morning, shall I? We can read some stories and then maybe play a game or two."

"Yes. Come early."

"After breakfast," she said gently.

He nodded and flung his arms around her. "Thank you," he said.

Rashid was surprised. Mo was not usually demonstrative.

Bridget hugged him back and then walked quickly to the door, "Until tomorrow then. Good night."

"Good night," Mo said.

Rashid rested his hand on his son's head for a moment. "Go to sleep when Alaya says it's time. I'll see you tomorrow as well."

Rashid opened the door for Bridget, and called Alaya back into the room.

"Allow me to show you to the solarium," he said after he bade his son good night.

"I would appreciate it. Do you normally give guests a road map? This place is huge," she asked lightly.

"My apologies, I had thought Francesca would show you the way."

"Maybe she stopped by. I took a shower, and took longer dressing than I planned. That's why I'm late."

He deliberately blocked the image of Bridget Rossi in the shower, water streaming down her womanly body, her hair darkened with the spray. The freckles would stand out against her pale skin. Did she have them elsewhere, or only that enchanting dusting across her nose?

"You won't have time for a cocktail," he said, reining in his thoughts.

"That's not a problem. I hope I haven't held up the rest of your guests."

"I'm sure they started without us." Since they were for the most part longtime friends who had the run of the house when they visited, Rashid wasn't concerned.

The solarium was at the end of the house, beyond the grand salon. It seemed full of people when Bridget and Rashid first stepped in. She looked quickly for Francesca, spotting her with a tall, gangly man who looked totally bemused. There seemed to be more than the half a dozen Rashid said were staying with him.

"There you are, darlings," Francesca said, advancing on them, ignoring the young man left standing midsentence.

"I didn't know the way," Bridget said brightly. "Luckily I ran into Rashid on the stairs."

"And why are you so late?" Francesca asked Rashid. "It's almost time for dinner."

"Business."

"What else? Honestly, you are on vacation, let someone else handle things," she said, smiling. "We have to work on your tendency to put duty before everything else."

"What would you have me do, ignore it?" he asked.

"There's a time and a place for everything."

Bridget smiled, remembering the time they'd been on vacation and Francesca had left in a heartbeat when a coveted assignment had appeared.

Just then a chime sounded.

"Charles, would you escort Francesca in?" Rashid called to the young man Francesca had been talking with.

"I wish to introduce Bridget to my grandmother before dinner. We will join you momentarily." He slipped from beneath her grasp and cupped Bridget's elbow. "Come."

The other guests smiled and called greetings as Rashid led Bridget to a chair near the side of the solarium. An elderly woman dressed in black sat in solitary splendor. She was gazing tranquilly over the blossoms now visible beneath artificial lighting in the garden.

"Grandmother, may I present my guest, Bridget Rossi? Bridget, my mother's mother Salina al Besoud."

The woman smiled at her grandson then looked sharply at Bridget. "Rossi? Related to Francesca?"

"She's my cousin."

"Hmm."

Bridget blinked. Usually people told her how lucky she was to have such a beautiful cousin. She wasn't sure how to respond.

"It's nice to meet you," she said politely.

"How long are you here for?" The older woman rose as she said it, and reached for the arm Rashid held for her.

"As long as she likes. Bridget just buried her father. I thought visiting with her cousin would help the transition before she returns home to San Francisco,'' he replied before Bridget could.

''Ah, you are from America. Tell me about your home. Is it true San Francisco is always bathed in sunshine?'' Madame Besoud asked.

Arriving at the dining room, Bridget was seated next to Salina al Besoud with Francesca on her right.

Rashid made the introductions. Bridget greeted Jack and Marie almost as old friends. Charles Porter gave her a brief greeting. Elizabeth Wainswright, sitting opposite Francesca, seemed very unhappy and barely nodded. Everyone spoke English for which Bridget was grateful.

''Jack and Charles and I were in school together in England. We still get together every chance we get,'' Rashid explained.

As the dinner progressed, however, it became clear that though they all spoke the same language, Bridget had nothing else in common with the other guests. She listened as Francesca held court with her delightful stories about the world of haute couture. Elizabeth spoke briefly about plans to visit Paris after she left Aboul Sari.

Jack broke in with talk about polo matches. At which point he challenged the gentlemen to a match while they visited so the other guests could see Rashid in action.

"You are quiet," Rashid's grandmother said to Bridget as the meal wound down.

She smiled. "I have nothing to contribute."

The older woman studied her for a moment then looked down the length of the table. "Neither does anyone else. I do believe they talk only to hear themselves."

Bridget stifled a giggle. Some of the inanities Jack spouted could be thought that. Charles had said little, gazing like a love-struck gazelle at Francesca.

Bridget smiled when the agreement made to play a polo match before the guests departed was struck. She would love to see a match, and wondered if there were somewhere she could get a book on the intricacies of the game.

"Do you follow polo?" Rashid's grandmother asked.

"No, I've never seen it played but it sounds exciting."

"What do you do with your time?"

"I'm a librarian in San Francisco."

"What happened to your father?"

Bridget spent a few moments quietly telling Madame al Besoud about her father's death and burial. How Rashid had come to the funeral with Francesca and ended up inviting her to his home. When she came to the part about reading to Mo the next day, the woman evidenced surprise. The first emotion Bridget had seen her display.

"Perhaps you could read to me as well," the woman said. "I speak English but reading it is more difficult. A friend sent me a book, I should like to write back to tell her that I enjoyed it."

"I would be happy to. What book?"

''*Four Hole Swamp*. It's a murder mystery. My friend loves them, but I don't always understand why.''

''I've heard of that book. It's supposed to be very good. I should like to read it with you.''

''Come to my apartment after lunch tomorrow. Unless you need to lie down then.''

''No, I don't.'' Bridget smiled at the idea of taking a nap every day. She was too busy at work and taking care of her father. Suddenly she remembered. She would never have that task again.

Rashid's grandmother reached out and patted her hand. ''The grief gets easier with time.''

Bridget blinked back tears. ''I know. My mother died a few years ago. I still miss her, but it does get easier. But I've always had Papa, and to know I'll never hear his laugh, or feel his arms tight in a hug is almost more than I can bear.''

''I still miss my father and he died thirty years ago,'' Salina al Besoud said softly.

"But now I have happy memories that bring me comfort. Think of the happy times."

Dinner ended with the house party returning to the solarium. Soft music played. A table had been set up for cards. Bridget paused in the doorway and sought Rashid. She was too tired to stay and hoped he didn't think she was being rude by retiring early.

She saw her cousin and crossed the wide room.

"I'm going to go to bed," she said softly. "Do you think Rashid will think I'm rude to cut out early?"

"Not at all. Sleep well. Tomorrow we'll catch up on all our news."

Rashid came up to them. "Thinking of retiring?" he asked.

She nodded, suddenly feeling awkward. No one else seemed ready to leave. She hoped he would put it down to grief and not a longing to be by herself for a while, though she needed the time alone.

"Sleep well, then, Bridget. And thank you for your kindness to my son."

"What kindness?" Francesca asked. "When did you meet his son?"

"Earlier. It's really nothing. I'm going to read him a book in the morning," Bridget said.

"Well we plan to spend most of the day by the pool. Come out to swim as soon as you can," Francesca said with a hug for her cousin. "A little sunshine will put roses in your cheeks."

Bridget had started up the stairs when Rashid called to her.

She turned. "Yes?" He'd followed her from the solarium.

"My grandmother told me of your offer to read to her. I didn't invite you here to entertain my family." He looked irritated.

"It's no problem. I love children and would like to spend some time with Mo. And your grandmother has a book we both would like to read, so why not together? Besides, it'll keep me from thinking about things. I do have to get on with life.''

''Wouldn't you rather spend the day by the pool with Francesca? And the others?''

''Not all day. Good grief, I'd look like a boiled lobster with my skin. Francesca tans beautifully, I burn and peel. Besides, I didn't bring a swimsuit. I didn't know I'd need one when I left home.''

''We have swimsuits in the changing room by the pool, as well as sunscreen and umbrellas,'' he said.

Standing just below her on the stairs their eyes were level. Bridget found herself mesmerized by her host. Her heart raced, her mind went numb.

''I'll be sure to check it out, then. And use both the sunscreen and umbrella,'' she said softly. What would he do if she leaned across the inches separating them and kissed him?

What would she do if she lost her mind enough to try?

Turning she almost scampered up the stairs before she made an idiot of herself with a man she'd just met that morning.

*   *   *

Rashid watched her hurry up the stairs and head down the corridor to her room. His hand tightened on the banister to keep himself from following her. To make sure she had everything she needed.

To see if he'd just imagined the spark of awareness that threatened to burst into flames when he stood near her.

CHAPTER THREE

RASHID entered Mo's room the next day mid-morning, startled to find it empty. He called for Alaya.

"Sir?" She appeared in the door from the adjoining room.

"Where is Mo?"

"Miss took him to the gardens. They were going to read books in English," she said. "Should I have told them not to?" She looked worried.

"Where in the gardens?"

"I don't know. I told them to be back in time for lunch."

He nodded once, curtly, and left. Alaya followed him into the hall. "Shall I go find them?"

"I'll look for them myself."

Rashid had no idea where they'd be, but they couldn't have gone far. Mo was a little boy and Bridget didn't know the grounds. Ten minutes later, he was baffled. He hadn't found them anywhere.

He even swung by the pool area to see if they'd gone there. Marie and Francesca were lying on chaise longues, but there was no sign of his son or Bridget.

He was about to concede defeat and call in help from the gardeners when he heard Mo's laugh. Following the sound, he found them both up a tree!

Fists at his waist, he gazed up into the wide branches of an old cedar. Snuggled together on a wide, sturdy branch near the trunk, Bridget and Mo were laughing at a picture in a book balanced on her lap.

''What are you doing up there?'' he asked.

Mo peered down. ''Hello, Father. Bridget and I went exploring and found this perfect hide way.''

''Hideaway,'' she corrected. She peeped through the leaves. ''He's safe. I wouldn't let him fall. We're not really that high.''

"And you couldn't have read the story just as easily sitting on a bench?"

"Where's your sense of adventure? Wouldn't you've rather been in a tree than on a bench when you were five?"

He stared at her. What had he been doing when he was five? Certainly not climbing trees. He'd had a tutor and was cooped up inside learning his letters and numbers.

"Maybe you're right. Can you two get down? It's almost time for lunch."

"We may need some help," she confessed, looking at the stack of books beside her. "How about I drop the books down to you and then help Mo climb down?"

"Fine."

He easily caught the storybooks she tossed down, placing them beside him. Reaching up, he lifted his son down and put him on the ground next to the books. "You pick them up and carry them to the house," he instructed.

Turning back, Rashid reached up to help Bridget descend.

She landed in a flurry, her hands on his arms, his hands on her waist. For a moment they stared at each other, awareness shimmering between them.

Rashid wanted to draw her closer, feel the soft curves of her body against his. Learn the sweet taste of her mouth. See if the desire that erupted was ephemeral or lasting. He'd only met her yesterday, yet he felt a strong pull of attraction he hadn't felt in a long time. Not since Fatima had died.

He slowly pulled her closer.

''Can we read tomorrow, Bridget?'' Mo asked, shattering the moment. He looked up trustingly at Bridget.

Rashid stepped back, dropping his hands to his sides. How could he have forgotten Mo?

''Bridget may have other things to do tomorrow,'' he said to his son, avoiding his guest's eyes. Hopefully she saw nothing amiss in his helping her down.

''Unless your father has plans for his guests, I don't see why not. I'll let you know before bed, okay?'' she said, smiling brightly at his son. Rashid flicked her a glance, wishing she'd turn that smile his way.

''Okay,'' Mo said happily.

Rashid nudged Mo's shoulder. ''What do you say to Bridget for reading to you?''

''Thank you!'' Mo gave a big whoop. ''It was so much fun. I should like to do this every day!''

''I would, too,'' Bridget said.

Rashid was certain he imagined a wistful note in her tone. Women liked excitement and adventure, not spending time with little boys. What was her game?

''Run along to Alaya, Mo. She will have your lunch ready for you soon.''

''Okay! Bye, Bridget.'' He gave her a brief hug again and headed happily up the path toward the house, carrying the half dozen books they'd read.

''Okay?'' Rashid queried.

''It's the new word I taught him. He is eager to learn,'' she murmured, brushing down her skirt. ''If I'm going to be climbing

trees again, I need some different clothes.''
She looked at Rashid. ''In fact, I'm going to
need some clothes just to complete the visit.
Do you suppose I could get a ride into town
and get some things at one of the shops?''

''I will put a car at your disposal.''

''Thank you. I thought Francesca might
like to go with me.''

''Perhaps Marie and Elizabeth would
round out the party and enjoy some of the
shops as well.''

When she hesitated, he knew instantly she
wanted time alone with her cousin.

''No, just Francesca,'' he said. ''Perhaps
tomorrow. I have to go to my offices in the
city, so I could drop you both and pick you
up later. Or I can arrange to have a car for
your own use.''

She smiled so brightly Rashid wished he
could have offered something more. What
would her smile be like presented with a di-
amond bracelet, he wondered.

''Thank you. That would be perfect. I'll
check with Francesca. I'll look forward to

seeing some of your capital city, as well. We whisked through it so fast yesterday I hardly had time to glimpse anything.'' She looked at her watch. ''Did you come to find us because it's almost lunchtime? I should clean up before joining the others.''

''You have plenty of time. Mo eats at noon. Our luncheon will be ready at one.'' Rashid started back toward the house, Bridget beside him.

''You have the most beautiful gardens,'' she said, pausing to smell one of the many blossoms that weighed down a bush. ''Mo and I walked around exploring. Then we tossed a stick in the pond to watch it float. Then we tried to name all the flowers. I recognized the roses and hibiscus, but you have many varieties I don't know. When we studied the shrubbery and trees, we found that one, so we just had to climb it. There's also a special hiding place behind one of the larger shrubs. Maybe we'll crawl in there for our next reading time.''

"Were you a tomboy as a child?" Rashid couldn't imagine any of the women of his acquaintance crawling into a special place made by bushes. But she made it sound adventurous and fun. No wonder Mo had been so happy.

"Not especially, mostly trying to keep up with Antonio. Though being sort of plain, I never was as caught up in makeup and fashion as Francesca. So I tried different activities."

"I would hardly describe you as plain." Had her father compared the two cousins and made Bridget feel less somehow? He knew his own father had employed that tactic with his sons, comparing them, urging them to excel in areas their brothers did not, in hopes of fostering strong men. Rashid didn't feel close to either brother as a result. If he had any other children, he would not take that tactic with Mo or his siblings.

"Well, I'm certainly not in Francesca's category. Even though she's two inches taller, I probably outweigh her by twenty pounds.''

He stopped and pulled her in front of him, his hands on her shoulders. The softness of her hair caressed the back of his fingers. She was not all skin and bone which he liked. He couldn't understand being worried about eating too much. She was perfect the way she was. Bridget Rossi was a vibrant woman. He suspected there was more to her than he saw on the surface.

His pulse pounded as he studied her. Her hair was fiery in the sun, not quite red, not brown, shot through with golden strands. Her eyes met his frankly, no guile or games there. The dusting of freckles across her nose were enchanting. He'd like to kiss every one.

Focus, he admonished himself. They were on a path in the garden, not some trysting place. People could wander down the path with no notice. Not to mention she was a guest in his home.

And he was not in line for a relationship at this point. Still, he was intrigued by this American.

''Sometimes there's a problem with people being too thin. Do you think a man likes to hold a woman who feels like she's anorexic? You are perfect just the way you are.''

She stared at him dumbfounded.

Slowly his fingers caressed her shoulders, feeling the toned muscles and soft skin beneath her cotton top. He wanted to feel her body against his, to test his theory, that she would be a perfect fit against him, that he would know he was holding an armful of femininity.

The urge to kiss her grew as each moment passed. She never blinked. Her eyes were wide and fathomless. Had he been the only one thinking of a kiss?

She was a guest in his home and he would not force himself on anyone but—

She stepped back, breaking contact.

''Thank you. I have never been told I was perfect before.'' She turned and hurried toward the house, much as she'd run up the stairs last night.

He began to walk after her, lengthening his stride until he caught up with her.

They came out of the bower of flowers just as Francesca and Marie were heading from the pool back to the house. The sarong skirt Francesca wore was gauzy and flowing, leaving her bikini top the only covering above her hips. Marie had covered herself from head to mid calf with a colorful caftan. Women were more circumspect in Aboul Sari than other countries in North Africa. Francesca knew that, so why did she ignore their custom, he wondered, irritated.

''The pool was fabulous,'' Marie called when she spotted them. She stopped to wait for them to catch up. Francesca also stopped, her expression definitely curious.

''I thought you were reading to Rashid's son this morning,'' she said as Bridget drew closer.

''I did. We had a delightful time. He's a sweet little boy. Funny, too. We found a tree to climb.''

Francesca smiled at that. ''Reminds me of when we were younger and you and Uncle Paolo came to visit.''

''Was the pool nice?'' Bridget asked.

''Lovely, but I don't want to get too tanned. I need to keep an even coloring for photos.''

Rashid listened to the interchange, glancing at Francesca. There was no denying she was beautiful to look at, but he couldn't help looking again at Bridget. She had a warmth and openness that called to anyone around her. A joie de vivre that was almost contagious.

''I thought you both might have joined us at the pool,'' Francesca said to Rashid.

''I had work to do, then I went to find Mo. He enjoyed Bridget's reading,'' he said.

''Maybe we can swim together this afternoon.''

''Sounds delightful.'' Not that he planned to spend the entire afternoon lounging by the pool, but swimming would be refreshing. And he needed to spend time with his guests—all of his guests, no matter how much he'd rather spend time with just one.

"Bridget wanted to do some shopping. Would you like to accompany her tomorrow?" he asked as they walked toward the double French doors opening off the solarium.

Francesca didn't hesitate a second. "I would love to. At that boutique you showed me last week?"

"If you like." It was a small, exclusive shop near the center of town. The proprietress had been delighted to have such a well-known fashion model patronize her establishment.

"I do." Francesca's mood seemed to swing to happiness instantly. Cynically Rashid knew it wasn't all due to the promise of more time with her cousin, but the idea of shopping for more new dresses. He'd never known anyone so interested in clothes as Francesca.

She looked at Bridget. "You'll love the boutique, the clothes are fantastic. I assume you won't be coming with us tomorrow,'' Francesca said to Rashid.

He shook his head. ''The last time I went with you, I had to spend my entire time fending off giggles and odd looks from the saleswomen. You and Bridget will enjoy yourself more without me.''

Francesca laughed. ''We would have more fun just the two of us.'' She linked arms with Bridget and started walking toward the house. ''We'll buy the place out!''

Rashid walked with Marie, his gaze drawn to the two in front of them. He had other guests to see to, he couldn't devote his entire time to the cousins. But for a moment, he wished he could see Bridget trying on a variety of dresses at the boutique.

It was midmorning before Francesca was ready to leave the next day. Rashid had left early, sending the car back for the ladies. Bridget had gone out onto the steps at the appointed time and was waiting for her cousin. She almost went back to find

Francesca, when she swept out, dressed in a white linen dress that looked stunning with her recent tan and dark hair. Bridget felt a swell of happiness at the thought of spending time just the two of them.

She wished she could find a way to casually find out if there was something more between her host and her cousin than friendship. She'd watched them yesterday when everyone was together and hadn't detected any special bond between them. But what if she were starting to grow interested in a man her cousin was also interested in?

"Have you known Rashid long?" Bridget asked.

"A couple of years or so. He came to one of the charity events I was modeling at and we met. He's fun, isn't he?"

"Yes." Fun, exciting, mysterious and so sexy she was having erotic dreams at night.

"Sad about his wife," Francesca said.

"He said she died."

"It's always sad when someone like that dies so young. Why can't criminals die young?" Francesca said.

''He said she was beautiful.''

''I don't know, I never met her, but I can't imagine him not wanting someone as beautiful as he himself is.''

Bridget nodded, feeling her heart drop. Or course a man that handsome would like to have an equally beautiful companion. Someone like Francesca?

''So are the two of you...?'' Bridget trailed off, hoping Francesca knew what she was asking.

Her cousin laughed. ''Not at all. We're friends. I have lots of friends, but no one special—maybe one day. But, Bridget, we need to enjoy today together. The reason I was late is my agent called—there's this fantastic opportunity.''

''Not again,'' Bridget said. ''The last time we tried to vacation together you left.''

''I know. I'll make it up to you. But this is a special event featuring Versace originals. I can't turn it down.''

''So when do you leave?''

"Tomorrow, if I can get a flight out. The next day at the very latest, and then I'd have no time to rest before the fittings and rehearsals."

"I'll have to leave, then," Bridget said slowly. She had just arrived, gotten a taste of the exotic lifestyle so foreign to her own.

"Nonsense, Rashid invited you for a couple of weeks."

"I don't know him. I can't stay. It was one thing with you here, but I can't stay on my own."

"Of course you can," Francesca said. "He'll insist, you watch."

"I doubt it. And if so, only to be polite."

"It seems to me every time I turn around there you are in private conversation with Rashid," Francesca said. "I'm sure an extended invitation won't be for politeness."

Francesca raised her hand, pointing to the index finger of her left hand with the index finger of her right. "First the night you arrived, the two of you were chummy when you walked into the solarium. Second—" she touched the next finger "—you and he were walking around the garden together yesterday. You said you'd been reading to his son, but I saw no little boy. Third—" another finger "—last night you and he were sure cozy with his grandmother until we called him to join us at cards."

"You are imagining things. We've spent a short time together every time you've seen us." They had not had private conversations. Not really. A time or two, maybe, but only because they'd been alone. It wasn't as if it meant anything.

At least, not to Rashid. Bridget looked out the window. She remembered every word Rashid had said. Her excitement for the shopping expedition had waned. She and Francesca had such a limited time to visit they should be sitting somewhere private and catching up. But Francesca was already talking again about the boutique they would visit.

"I'm not here to spend time with Rashid, I came to spend time with you. I'm glad we're shopping just the two of us. I was afraid Marie or Elizabeth would join us. This is your field of expertise, I hope you can help me pick out some dresses that will really suit me,'' Bridget said, resigned to the inevitable.

''Leave everything to me. You'll want to get a special dress for the reception next week,'' Francesca said, reaching out to squeeze Bridget's hand.

''What reception?''

''There's some state affair that Rashid invited us to attend. His father is actually the host. It's in honor of a visiting ambassador. I expect there will be heads of state, officials from several countries as well as the elite of Aboul Sari. Since I won't be here, you'll have to represent the family. It'll knock your socks off.''

Bridget stared at her cousin. For a moment she remembered the last formal reception she'd attended, with Richard Stewart, the man she'd been dating at the time. He'd been up for partnership in the prestigious law firm he worked in, and they'd been invited to a

very formal event at the senior partner's home.

Bridget almost shivered in remembrance.
Richard had been furious after the accident.
She had not tried to ruin his chances, as he'd
claimed. Someone had bumped her arm and
the glass of red wine had seemed to float out
of her hand.

She'd tried to explain to him, but he hadn't
listened at all. And her hostess had been less
than gracious, making her feel even more
clumsy and inept. White dress, white brocade
love seat, white carpet, all with a dark red
wine stain.

Bridget had vowed never to attend an important, formal affair again. Yet her cousin
was thrilled with the idea.

"I think I'd have a heart attack." She'd
never be comfortable as long as she could
hear Richard's verbal tirade echo in her mind.

"You'll have a fabulous time. Live a little!
Too soon you'll have to return to San
Francisco and your regular life. When will
you vacation here again?"

That was some of the problem. This vacation was like a fantasy. She was swept up in the wonder of it all. Not forgetting her father, but able to put things in perspective and begin to move on.

This morning, she'd looked in on Mo, promising to find him when she returned from shopping to read to him again. She'd have to ask Rashid if the little boy could swim. They could play in the pool together if so. She would enjoy that more than lying in the sun doing nothing. That allowed too much time for sad thoughts.

When they reached the boutique, the chauffeur slid to a stop before the small shop and escorted them to the entrance.

"Welcome." A small woman met them, bowing in greeting and opening the door wide. "I am honored to have you favor my shop," she said, smiling at Francesca.

"I brought my cousin with me today," Francesca said walking through to the elegant love seats in the center of the room. Several gowns were displayed along the wall, but the shop looked nothing like the stores Bridget normally patronized.

Bridget glanced around and followed her cousin. Sitting on the love seat opposite Francesca, she felt awkward. Were there only a half a dozen dresses for sale? None of them looked practical for her.

"We are looking for some clothing for my cousin. She arrived unexpectedly and didn't bring enough dresses for a visit with Sheikh al Halzid," Francesca recounted as another young woman entered, carrying a heavy silver tray loaded with sweets, biscuits, a lavish teapot and paper-thin cups.

"Resort wear?" the woman asked.

"That and a couple of dresses for dinner and something for a formal reception," Francesca said. She looked at Bridget and winked. "Maybe something casual for playing with children."

Bridget smiled at her cousin.

"But nothing too extravagant," Bridget said.

Francesca laughed. "Don't worry about the bill, it's taken care of. I'm happy to share this time with you."

Dresses and pants, shorts and swimsuits were paraded before them. Some Bridget loved, others shocked her, she would never wear such clothes. But she was charmed with the genuine desire of the saleswomen to find just the right attire for her.

Francesca picked out most of the dresses for Bridget, commenting on what went with her coloring. She then chose a couple to try on herself. Bridget was overwhelmed with her cousin's generosity. She wanted to keep an eye on costs. Only, there were no tags on anything. Which probably didn't matter, she didn't understand the country's currency so wouldn't really know how much something cost.

An older woman rapped on the front door of the establishment. One of the saleswomen quickly went to speak to the woman standing outside. The exchange was in Arabic, so

Bridget hadn't a clue what was said, but the woman left in a huff.

"Was that another customer?" Bridget asked Francesca quietly.

"Probably. She'll come back. Time to try on these things, to make sure they fit."

"Why not come in now and look around?" Bridget persisted.

"Because we are here, of course. Rashid arranged for an exclusive showing. The boutique is closed to others as long as we are here."

Bridget was astonished. "They can do that?"

"They are doing it. His business is important to them. They'll do whatever he asks. Go try on that aqua dress. That color looks great on you."

Bridget followed the younger salesclerk into the dressing room. It was the size of her bedroom at home. Floor-length mirrors lined one wall, a free-standing full-length mirror stood nearby, to enable a customer to see the back as well as the front of any creation she tried on.

And that's what Bridget felt like. She was trying on creations, not mere dresses. The materials felt soft and sensuous against her skin. The aqua color did wonders for her, making her skin seem even fairer and her eyes a deeper blue. She liked the way the dress fit.

The rose shirtwaist felt luxurious, and the color looked surprisingly good despite her hair. She wouldn't have tried it without Francesca's urging.

It was an hour later by the time she tried on the last dress the woman had brought. It was a confection, no other word for it. A rich cream color, the single shoulder bodice felt as if it were a specially designed body suit, fitting snugly, yet allowing ease of movement. The long skirt swirled around her legs. She loved walking in it, feeling like a princess must feel when everything in the world was perfect.

She couldn't imagine anything better for the reception that loomed. If Francesca would be generous enough to extend to this one, she'd be thrilled. If not, she'd splurge and buy it herself, no matter what the cost.

"Francesca, wait until you see this!" She swept into the main salon. But Francesca wasn't there. Rashid was.

He sat on one of the love seats, making it seem absurdly frail and feminine. He rose when she entered and let his gaze travel from her head to her toes.

"Exquisite," he said softly.

"Oh." Bridget didn't know what to say. Her heart rate increased. For a split second she was delighted he could see her in the dress. It was the prettiest thing she'd ever worn. Even if she never wore it again, Rashid had seen her and thought her exquisite.

The salesclerk hovered nearby, reaching out to adjust the dress where no adjustment was needed. She spoke rapidly to Rashid in Arabic and he nodded.

"I have told her that dress is definitely a keeper. She will include it with the others you've chosen. Are you almost ready to return to the villa?"

"Yes. I'll change right away."

"No hurry. Francesca is trying something on."

But Bridget had enough. The pile of clothes that had accumulated would give her more than enough for her stay. She was thrilled with the selections and knew she had her cousin to thank for helping her choose colors and styles she would have hesitated to try on her own.

Dressing in one of the new skirts and tops, she rejoined Rashid in the main salon as soon as she was able.

"I wanted to thank you for making this day so wonderful," she said, sitting primly opposite him on the matching love seat. "I never had a store close to others just so I could see the clothes. It's been fabulous! Did you get some tea? They served us tea earlier. The salesclerks seemed to know my size just by looking at me. Not a single thing I tried on didn't fit. Some I didn't like on as well as off, but they all fit perfectly.''

''And you found enough to tide you over until you return home?'' he asked.

''More than enough. I even found a darling swimsuit, with a modest coverup. I wanted to ask you if Mo swims and if so would you trust him with me? We could use the pool when your guests aren't there, so we wouldn't bother them.''

He raised an eyebrow. ''I was under the impression you were also one of my guests, Bridget Rossi. How can you and Mo use the pool when no guests are there?''

''But I am not bothered by your son. He said he has strict orders not to bother any one. I know others don't always want to be around kids like I do, but he's so delightful.''

''If I suggest you spend more time with Francesca?''

''I'm happy to spend all my time with her, but she just told me she has to leave for an assignment.'' Bridget took a breath. She'd almost forgotten. "I should probably leave as well."

"No, stay and enjoy yourself a bit. Refresh yourself before returning home. The duties and sad tasks will await," he said.

"Unless Antonio has already started with the estate. He is the executor. Maybe he can wind everything up before I return." It wasn't fair to leave everything to her brother, but she wasn't up to the tasks just yet.

She looked at her new skirt. "Do you think I'm frivolous shopping so soon after Papa died?"

"Not at all. One of the hard things to deal with after a family member dies is the fact life goes on. Would your father have wanted you to stop everything for a period of time to mourn him?"

"Of course not. He loved life. He was always encouraging me to try new things, learn to skate, try rowing, things like that. I wish you could have known him, he was so special."

"I wish I had, as well. You speak highly of him. As does Francesca," Rashid said.

"He doted on her, but she rarely came to visit. We mostly saw her as a child when we visited Italy. Are you sure you want me to stay?"

"I am most definitely sure."

Bridget looked at him, caught up in the dark gaze that seemed to hold her in thrall. Her skin grew warm as her heart rate increased. She felt that shaft of awareness again, and for a moment the elegant boutique faded. The world only contained Rashid.

She shook her head, as if breaking a spell. Looking away, she took a deep breath. "I don't want to impose. But if you're sure, then let me know about Mo's swimming. Being with him helps cheer me up!"

"Ah, your universal excuse when I suggest my family is imposing on you," Rashid said.

"You kindly invited me to visit to help in the transition over my father's death," she reminded him.

He inclined his head once.

"Certainly spending time with a child is the best way to do that. A young life with so much ahead of him."

"So how does my grandmother fit in?" he asked.

"That's for fun." She thought about it for a moment. "And for wisdom. She is a wise woman, I think. And gracious in her time with me."

"You gave her pleasure explaining the problematic sections of the book yesterday. She looks forward to your reading more with her."

"As do I."

He leaned forward, closing the distance between them. "Is it enough, Bridget, to help you forget? I can make a car available for you to explore, take you to the beach, share some of the treasures of my country, accompany you to parties and receptions. You should not spend your vacation doing what you would do at home."

"Trust me, Rashid, I never do things like this at home. But I wouldn't say no to a tour of historic sites, or even a view of the beach. Does Mo like the beach?''

Rashid narrowed his gaze slightly. ''I don't believe I know if he does or doesn't.''

Before Bridget could react to that startling statement, Francesca swept into the room, making a definite entrance, wearing a flame-red slip dress that hugged her slim frame like a second skin.

''Rashid, I didn't know you'd arrived. What do you think?'' She twirled around, assumed a sultry pose and walked toward him like she was on a catwalk in Milan.

He rose and studied her. ''It's beautiful with your coloring and figure,'' he said.

She continued toward him until she almost touched him, flirting as she trailed a red tipped finger along his jaw. ''I want you to think I'm beautiful in it. A model has to be beautiful, or she loses work.''

''You are always beautiful, Francesca,'' he replied.

She smiled, glancing at Bridget. ''Did you get everything you wanted?''

"Yes, thank you. I'm set for the rest of my stay and then some."

"If you are ready to return to the villa, I'll wait. If not, I'll send the car back for you," Rashid said.

"We about bought out the place. I'll just change. Won't be a minute. Then we'll ride back with you and after lunch we can go to the pool. Wait until you see the swimsuit I just bought."

Rashid sat back on the love seat, his eyes once again on Bridget. "She has a love of fine things."

Bridget nodded, wishing their time together wasn't going to be so short. She had some more questions for her cousin—all centering on Rashid.

"She always looks good in anything she wears," Bridget said wistfully.

"That's her job. She wouldn't be a very effective model if she didn't."

Bridget had to believe Francesca's saying the two of them were just friends. Rashid certainly didn't sound that besotted with her cousin.

"I have other commitments tomorrow, but the day after I would be happy to show you some of our historic sights. To view all the ones we treasure in our country would take much longer than a day, I'm afraid," Rashid said. "Though we will see all we can while you are here."

"I should love to see whatever we can in the time you can allot. I haven't been to as many places as Francesca, as I'm sure you know, so this is all wonderfully new to me," Bridget said enthusiastically. Many of the buildings she'd seen were old, with lovely designs and carvings. The entire city had a different feel from San Francisco. She'd love to explore more—especially with Rashid.

"You live in one of the world's loveliest cities. Tell me about your life in San Francisco," he invited.

Bridget knew he was only being polite, but he was her host, so she would comply. She gave him a brief background about growing up as the child of a restauranteur, of helping out in the restaurant during high school and college for extra money. How she'd settled in her flat with the narrow view of the Bay if she leaned out the bedroom window. What aspects she liked best about her job as a librarian. How on occasion she'd act as hostess for her father, less and less as the years had gone by and he'd cut back on activities, turning the day to day running of the restaurants over to Antonio.

''You mention friends from time to time,'' Rashid commented, ''But never one special male friend. You do not have one?''

She shook her head, thinking of Richard. She hadn't found anyone since that episode that she wanted to develop a relationship with. Did it look as if she couldn't attract the attention of one special man? Suddenly she wished her cousin would hurry up so they could leave. She didn't like being reminded that next to Francesca, she was a definite also-ran.

"Sorry, I had to try on one more dress," Francesca said as she breezed into the salon. "Ready?"

"We were just waiting for you," Bridget said, jumping up.

"I was about to tell your cousin the men in San Francisco must be blind and crazy to let someone as lovely as she is remain single for so long," Rashid said also rising.

CHAPTER FOUR

DID Bridget really wish to leave since her cousin was departing early, or was she just being polite, Rashid wondered as they drove back to the villa together. They had not done much in the three days she'd been visiting. Maybe he should make an effort to show her more of the delights his country had to offer.

And learn a bit more about the woman while he was at it.

The clothing purchases were being sent and should arrive at the villa before the end of the day. Rashid reviewed what activities he'd planned for his guests for this afternoon. A few hours at the pool, then time with Jack and Charles for a game of billiards while the women fussed and got ready for dinner.

Charles and Jack were counted among his closest friends, but suddenly Rashid felt their visit had gone on long enough. He almost resented the time he had to spend with his friends. He wanted to spend it with Bridget.

Fatima had doted on their son. Had she lived, he was certain they would have had more children. She seemed happiest when with Mo.

Bridget also liked being with his son. Americans viewed the whole love and marriage situation differently. Was there such a thing as enduring love? What would marriage be like to someone who you truly loved?

His parents had a respectful relationship. He knew they cared for him and his brothers.

His grandmother's life had not been that happy, but she had never complained in his hearing.

And he and Fatima had always been compatible. She had taken care of their home, been a suitable hostess and given him Mo. He'd grown to love her as the years passed. And he missed her, but not with a gut-wrenching feeling that wouldn't end. He would always regret she had died so young. Moving on had seemed impossible for a time, but he had done so. Would he risk developing feelings for another? He had a son, and he was content with his life as it was.

Yet, there was something about Bridget Rossi that intrigued him beyond anything he'd ever felt before.

He leaned forward to see Bridget. She was gazing out the car window at the building they were passing. He knew if he sent his other guests packing, she'd leave as well.

Maybe he should give her a further incentive to remain.

''I hope you plan to attend the reception my father is giving for the ambassador of Egypt. That last dress you tried on would be perfect,'' he said.

''Which dress?'' Francesca asked.

''I don't know if you saw it, the sales lady brought it into the dressing room. It's a cream-colored dress. Quite elegant, I think. But I'm not sure about going to the reception. I really don't care for events like that.'' Especially not after the fiasco with Richard. ''Anyway, I'm not the ambassador type,''

Bridget said, leaning forward to see him better. ''Thank you for asking me.''

''Everyone at the villa will be going, so you'll know some people there. Many others who will be there also speak English. Plan to attend,'' he said.

Bridget suppressed a desire to snap a salute at his imperial tone. ''I'll see,'' she hedged.

Francesca laughed. ''That used to mean no, when your mother said it.''

Bridget nodded, remembering how they knew exactly what her mother had meant. From there her thoughts turned to the relationship between her parents. Her mother had loved her father so much, and Papa had never loved her in return. It had been expedient for him to marry—for the sake of his young son. But she wondered why he couldn't have at least pretended to love his second wife.

She couldn't decide if that would have been worse. But how could anything be worse than to love someone, make a life and family with him, and know in his eyes, it was only second best?

She shouldn't be thinking about old family dynamics with Rashid sitting there. Nothing would change the past. She had a more current situation to consider—if he was serious about her attending the reception. What in the world would she do at some state reception? She'd be so tongue-tied and shy she'd be miserable. Not to mention worried she'd dump wine or something worse in the ambassador's lap! She'd have to find a way to decline.

Even the thought of wearing her beautiful dress to the reception wasn't enough. She'd be totally out of her depth. She might dream of fancy balls and romantic nights but truth to tell, she'd be too worried to enjoy it.

Luncheon was more informal than previous meals, with the staff serving it on the patio next to the pool. Marie and Elizabeth had been swimming during the morning and donned their coverups for the meal.

''You are joining us this afternoon, right, Rashid?'' Marie asked.

"We all are, I believe," he said, glancing around the group.

"How about a look at the stables, old man," Jack said. "I'd rather go there than swim. Have to see if you have enough horses for the match."

The polo match had been scheduled for Saturday, and Jack wanted a chance to practice beforehand with a couple of Rashid's mounts.

"We can do both. Visit the stables first then join the ladies for a swim. Would anyone else care to join us?"

Francesca shook her head. Marie responded with a quick, "No thank you, I've seen horses before." Elizabeth accepted. Bridget wished she could accept as well, but knew she couldn't keep up with their conversation about polo. Besides, she'd rather spend time with Francesca before she left in the morning.

During lunch, Charles boasted a bit about his prowess on the polo field and before long, he and Jack were trying to outshine each other with tales of their exploits. Bridget found it funny the two men were so adamant about a game. But she knew how men were about football in the States, and figured it was some universal gene they all shared.

Once everyone had finished eating, the men and Elizabeth headed for the stables. Francesca, Marie and Bridget settled in beside the pool. Bridget chose a chaise in the shade of a large umbrella, wishing her swimsuit had arrived so she could swim.

Francesca sat in the chair beside Bridget. "Tell me what your plans are when you return home. Will you help Antonio in the restaurants or what?"

"I'll continue in my job. I was never that enthusiastic about business. And the only thing I was good at in the restaurants was waiting tables. Antonio will probably make the restaurants even bigger than Papa did. He loves them as much."

"Isn't this place grand?" Francesca said looking around. "I love being here. This is my second visit. I think it's become my favorite place to vacation. I really lap up this luxury. It's so different from my real life.''

''And that being?'' Bridget asked.

''I know you think being a model is glamorous, but it's darn hard work. And I sure wish I could eat like you do. When I finally am ready to give it up, I expect to grow as large as Aunt Louisa,'' she said, mentioning their largest relative.

Bridget gave her a glance. ''I doubt it. Your mother is not heavy, why should you be?''

''I plan to eat my way through everything I've had to deny myself these last years to stay thin. Speaking of which, I need to go up and pack. See you in a bit.''

Bridget dozed for a while, relishing the delightful setting. The warm air caressed her skin gently as the breeze moved across. The water shimmered in the sunshine. The colorful hibiscus and gardenias that segregated the pool area added color and fragrance to a perfect setting.

Time drifted by and Bridget began to feel restless.

A shadow crossed her face and she opened her eyes. Rashid stood beside the chaise, blocking the sun.

"Your clothes have arrived," he said softly.

She sat up, noticing Marie was fast asleep beneath another umbrella.

"I thought you might wish to see them again," he said, offering a hand to help her rise.

"Finished at the stable?" she asked.

"Yes. You should have come."

"Maybe sometime when polo afficionados aren't around."

"We wouldn't have talked polo the entire time."

She smiled up at him, then hesitated as his eyes darkened.

"Come, show me what you bought," he said, taking her arm.

When they stepped inside her room a few moments later, Marsella was busy unpacking the bags piled on the bed.

She smiled and said something in Arabic. The wardrobe door stood open with several dresses already hung. Bridget couldn't help contrasting the available space with the few articles she'd brought.

Shyly, Bridget held up each new dress or skirt, holding them against her as she watched Rashid's reaction. She remembered doing so for her father many times as a teenager, but Rashid was very different from her father. And she was no longer a teenager.

Rashid was a very appreciative audience, urging her to try on one or two dresses and model for him. She slipped into the bathroom and donned the first dress—the aqua one she'd liked so much. Stepping out, she tried to emulate her cousin. It was like playing dress-ups and to her surprise, once her initial shyness faded, Bridget enjoyed every moment. She wasn't sure she could ever be a model for a crowd of critical viewers, but for an appreciative audience of one, it was terrific.

Lastly she changed into her swimsuit and pulled on her cover-up. This would not be a part of the impromptu fashion show. When she stepped out of the bathroom, she noted his glance, felt her skin heat even more at the male appreciation she saw in his eyes when his gaze slid down her legs. Thankfully the cover-up was as modest as a dress.

''I'm ready for that swim.''

''I'll join you in a few moments,'' Rashid said. ''We'll have the pool to ourselves, I think.''

''Then may we also take Mo?'' she asked.

Mo was happy to see her a few moments later and ecstatic when she offered to take him swimming. His nanny seemed in awe of Bridget, and hastened to help Mo change into a swimming suit.

The pool was deserted when they reached it. Rashid had been correct. They would have it to themselves. She shed her cover-up and went to the edge of the pool.

"Can you swim?" Bridget asked as she stepped down the stairs at the shallow end.

"Yes!" Mo launched himself off the side in a cannonball and splashed everywhere.

Bridget laughed when he bobbed up and began swimming furiously toward her. He was like a fish in water. She relaxed and plunged into the cool water, relishing the sensuous feel against her skin. She was going to adopt Francesca's attitude and enjoy the luxury while she could.

They played for a half hour before Rashid joined them. Sometimes they played tag. Then they had jumping contests to see who could make the biggest splash.

Mo laughed so hard after one of Bridget's jumps, she had to hold him up afraid he'd go under. Didn't his father play with him like that? She remembered how often she had played with her father. He may not have had a lot of love for her mother, but she had no questions he had loved her. He had made his children more important than anything in his life.

Rashid hunkered down near the side of the pool where Bridget was remembering.

"Are you ready to stop, or do I still have time to join you?"

To her disappointment, he had not already changed. "We have been having a great time. I taught Mo some new water games. Do join us."

"You are slightly pink. Should you be out this long?" Rashid asked, touching her shoulder lightly.

Bridget shivered at the touch. She looked up at him, caught in the dark gaze of his eyes. She had to swallow before she could reply.

"Probably not, but we're having fun."

"Still, I wouldn't want you to burn. Mo, swim to the side and I'll help you out. Next time I'll come immediately."

Mo did as his father asked, then turned to look at Bridget. "Can we go read a book?" Mo asked, dripping on the cement. "I don't want to go inside."

"We need to change." Bridget looked at the strong hand offered to her. Would he pull her out as easily as he had Mo?

She took the hand and in only an instant was streaming water on the cement as well. Rashid was only inches from her, his eyes holding her as if trying to convey some deeper meaning.

''Can you read me a book?'' Mo asked again.

''As long as we do it in the shade,'' she said, heading for the towels and her cover-up. She was ever conscious of the suit which had seemed so appropriate in the boutique and which now clung to her and revealed more than she'd like.

Quickly she wrapped one of the large towels around herself.

''The tree is in the shade,'' Mo called.

''So it is. How about the secret space behind the shrub?'' Rashid asked.

Mo looked at him, eyes wide. ''You know about that place?''

''I bet you and Bridget and I could fit in it with no trouble. I should like to hear Bridget read, as well. Both you and

Grandmother have had her take a turn, don't you think it's my turn now?''

Bridget looked at him. Her hair was wet and hung down around her shoulders. She knew she didn't have a speck of makeup on, and the sunscreen was failing if she was turning pink. Rashid wanted to spend time with her and Mo? Her heart kicked into high gear.

''You're on, though I bet it'll be crowded,'' she warned.

''Meet you both here in fifteen minutes.'' Rashid tousled his son's hair.

Bridget walked beside Mo feeling like a kid playing hooky or something. Rashid had five other guests, yet he planned to spend some time alone with her. And his son.

Twenty minutes later the three of them were weaving their way through the thick foliage. The space had seemed big enough when Bridget had first found it, but now with Rashid, it was definitely cozy. Mo claimed one spot, leaving Bridget to sit next to Rashid. Shoulders touched. His knee brushed against hers. Leaves filtered the sunlight, and a light breeze kept the air cool enough to enjoy.

Except for the heat generated by her own thoughts with him sitting so near.

Bridget reached for the first book, hoping her voice sounded normal when she read. Rashid sat so close, that when she turned her head, she could see the fine lines radiating from around his eyes. He wore casual attire which made him much more approachable than he'd ever seemed before. His shoulders were wide, his head just brushed the top of the space. His long legs stretched out drew her eye. She had to forcibly return her attention to the book, much as she'd rather stare at him. He was her host, nothing more.

"The Cat in the Hat," she began, reading the familiar rhyming story that brought such delight to so many children. Mo watched her avidly, as if absorbing the words through his eyes as well as ears.

"If you sit in Papa's lap, you can see the words as I read," she suggested after a few pages.

"Papa?" Rashid said.

Mo twisted his head to look at Rashid. "It's English. Bridget called her father that. It's …" He looked at Bridget with a question in his eyes. "Why do we call him Papa?"

"It's less formal than Father," Bridget said, looking at Rashid. "I hope you don't mind. He picked it up from my use."

"It's fine. Continue."

Mo happily clamored onto his father's lap, snuggling back so he could see the book when she tilted it slightly in his direction.

Rashid's hand came to rest on his son's hip, and he looked at Bridget, his eyes revealing nothing. "Do continue," he said.

The book was quickly read, along with the second one Mo had brought.

"The end," she finished, shutting the book and smiling at the little boy. He was fast asleep.

"Oops, guess swimming so long tired him out," she said softly. "Maybe we should take him inside."

"Crawling out of this bower would waken him," Rashid said, shifting a little, and holding his son close.

"I'm all for staying right here, if you are," she said wondering at her audacity. She knew he had other guests to see to, but she loved having his undivided attention for a short time.

"I've never done something like this," Rashid said softly, looking around the shady hideaway.

"You have the perfect grounds for children. Mo can run, climb, hide and make wonderful memories of a happy childhood. You should have a bunch."

"One needs to be married to have a bunch as you say," he replied.

"You can marry again, just ask your family," she said.

"Ask them what?"

"To arrange it."

He looked at her. "I'm capable of choosing my own wife."

"I thought you were a proponent of arranged marriages," she said.

"Not at all. They can work, they can not work. But when a man reaches a certain age, he's entitled to look where he wants for a wife."

"One suitable for his position," she said, as if to remind herself she would never be in the running. Not that she wanted to be. He was dangerous to her own peace of mind. She was on a vacation. She had come to experience a totally different scene before returning home to her life as it would be. She'd always miss her father, but this respite was helping her forget the worst of her sadness, and make new memories to enjoy when the loneliness encroached.

Besides, she had sworn to herself she would never be like her mother, second place to a memory. When and if she ever fell in love, it would be with a man who came to her wholehearted and unencumbered.

How would a woman marrying a widower with children ever know she was loved for herself and not for the help she could bring to run the family?

"Do you not believe a suitable marriage has a better chance to last than one that is unsuitable, or in which lust plays the primary role? What happens when that lust is assuaged and the novelty wears off?" he asked.

"I believe in lasting love. Love that doesn't wear off," she replied.

"Suitability plays no part?"

"Of course, to a degree. I don't think people fall in a forever love with someone who doesn't share the same values they do, or the same goals. But when I start to see some man, I want to envision him in fifteen years, with bratty teenagers around, or in thirty years, with receding hair and maybe a bit of a softness around the middle. Will I still want to be with him, share my life, my hopes? If so, then I'll know he's the right man," she said dreamily.

"No."

"No? No, what? That I won't believe he's Mr. Right?"

"I can't believe you meet a man and immediately start envisioning him in fifteen
years," he scoffed.

She laughed softly, reaching out to touch
Mo gently on his arm. "You're right. Only
if I think I might be seriously interested in
him."

"And so far not, right?"

"Oh, there've been one or two whom I
gave my fifteen-thirty-year test to. Neither
passed." Bridget looked at Rashid. Could she
envision him in fifteen years? In thirty? She
suspected he would not have receding hair,
nor a softness around the middle. She
couldn't envision him any different from the
way he was today—totally male, sexy as
could be, and so far from her universe as to
be almost a foreign species.

"What similar values would you want to
share with your Mr. Right?" Rashid asked.

"Family is important. And I hope to marry
a man who would want to have lots of kids.
I want a bunch. I only had one half brother

who was years older than me. I've always yearned to have brothers and sisters around.''

''What about parties, fancy clothes, jewelry?''

Bridget laughed. ''I hope we have lots of parties—barbecues with friends, others for family celebrations or holidays. I enjoyed lunch today. Everyone seemed to have a great time eating on the patio. That's the kind of party I like.''

''Formal receptions?''

''Scare me to death. Oops.'' She looked at him. ''Sorry, I was angsting over the reception next week. It's not my thing, really.''

''But you are going?''

She took a deep breath. ''If my host insists, I shall.''

''I do.''

''Will your grandmother be attending?''

''Of course. Her daughter is the hostess. Tell me more about your fantasy husband,'' he ordered.

Bridget wondered if he were trying to equate her fantasy man with the arranged marriages common in his country.

"I don't know. I don't have a list per se," she said.

"What about sex?"

"Well, yes. I hope there is some strong attraction between us. How do you think I'm going to get my bunch of kids," she asked with some asperity, embarrassed he brought up the topic. Especially when she had trouble not thinking of sex anytime she was around the man. He raised her hormone level every time he walked into the room.

Mo stirred and rolled over, falling off Rashid's lap and onto the ground, waking up.

He looked around. "Did you finish the book?"

"I did, young man. Time we were heading inside," Bridget said, glad for the interruption. The discussion was becoming too intimate for her comfort.

"Run along, Mo. Alaya will be wondering if you left home for good," Rashid said, lifting his son to his feet.

The little boy laughed and crawled from the shelter. Bridget followed and Rashid came behind her carrying the books. Mo scampered down the path. Rashid reached out his hand to stop Bridget from moving.

"Thank you for being kind to my son."

"No thanks necessary. He's a delight. Thank you for inviting me here, Rashid. It is helping. I know I still have to face what awaits me at home, but this time gives me a breather. I really appreciate it." Impulsively she reached up and gave him a brief kiss on the cheek.

He tossed the books down, and took her shoulders in his hands, drawing her against him, closing his mouth over hers.

CHAPTER FIVE

RASHID stood by the window in his grand-mother's sitting room and gazed out unsee-ing. She was finishing her breakfast and had asked to talk to him before the day started. She'd been speaking about the plans for the polo match but all he could focus on was the passionate kiss he'd given Bridget in the gar-den yesterday afternoon.

She'd been startled, but then, so had he. What possessed him to grab her like that, kiss her like that? Experimentation? To see if she was as sweet as she looked? To wantonly give into need and desire despite her status as guest?

Her kiss had been a polite thank-you. Could he excuse his as a thanks-for-reading-to-my-son? Hardly. A man didn't kiss a woman like he'd kissed Bridget as a thank-you.

It was more like a prelude to full body contact, under the covers, bare skin to bare skin.

He gave a soft groan as he thought about getting bare with Bridget. Her skin felt like velvet. What would it be like to touch every inch? Kiss her long into the night, nibbling on her, tasting the sweetness, feeling the heat they'd generate until he'd think they would burn up the sheets?

Even a man of his age could dream.

''Rashid!''

He turned. ''Yes?''

''Have you heard a single word I've said?'' His grandmother pushed aside the empty plate and pulled her cup and saucer closer. She took a sip of the hot chocolate as she watched her grandson with a puzzled expression.

''Something about a catered lunch at the grounds. The club house can provide what we need.''

''Is something wrong, my dear?'' she asked.

He shook his head. ''Just thinking about my guests and what entertainment I can provide.''

''All your guests or just one?'' she asked shrewdly.

Rashid wondered if his grandmother believed he was thinking about Francesca. Or did she suspect where his thoughts really lay—on Francesca's younger cousin? She was the first woman he felt intrigued by since Fatima died.

''Your mother is coming over this afternoon. We plan to gossip about the ambassador.''

He raised an eyebrow. ''I hardly think that is something I need to hear.''

She smiled secretly. ''I wanted to know if you were paying attention. I am concerned about your guests. I do not interfere with your life, but I feel I must say something this time. Elizabeth needs to step up and set Charles straight, or you do. His mooning over Francesca verges on being rude.''

"He's thirty-four years old, Grandmother. I don't think I can tell him how to behave." Jack had been married once, now divorced. He was widowed. Charles, however, had never seemed to step up to the commitment.

"I believe at dinner the first night he was here, he mentioned running for Parliament at the next election. He needs to get his priorities straight before such a move. If he can be swayed so easily by a pretty face, I don't hold out hope he'll succeed in public office," his grandmother said.

"Francesca is beautiful. Many men feel fortunate to spend time with her. I don't think it will affect how he deals in the British Parliament," Rashid said.

"I don't see Jack or you making a total idiot over the woman," she snapped.

No, but he could understand Charles' actions. He enjoyed looking at Francesca, she was lovely.

But not talking with her.

He frowned at the sudden insight. She didn't have much conversation that didn't revolve around fashion.

For a moment he wondered if he could begin to use Bridget's rule and envision himself
with Francesca in fifteen years? Or thirty
years. He couldn't even see them attending
the reception together.

But with Bridget—

"Rashid!"

"Yes?"

"Honestly what is wrong with you? That's
twice I've had to call you to pay attention.
You are worse than Mo. I will be tied up with
your mother. Bridget won't be reading to me
this afternoon, has she made plans with
Mo?"

"Actually, with Francesca leaving, I plan
to take Bridget sightseeing."

Salina al Besoud was silent for a long moment, staring nonplussed at her grandson. She
cleared her throat.

"Sightseeing?"

"She'd like to see some of our country
while she's here. No one else has evidenced
any interest, so I thought while everyone had
something else to do this afternoon, I'd show

her a bit of Aboul Sari. Maybe we'll even drive to the sea.''

''To the Med?''

''She would like to go to the beach. Though, I might make that an excursion for another day when we could take Mo with us. Do you know if he likes the beach?''

''I have no idea. Does it matter?'' She stared at him with confusion.

''You don't think it odd I don't even know that about my own son's likes and dislikes?'' Rashid asked.

''No. He's only five, what does he know?''

''I'm sure he has an opinion on a lot of things,'' Rashid said.

''Did Bridget ask if he liked the beach?''

Rashid nodded, wondering what else he didn't know about his son. He saw the boy infrequently. His work kept him from home during the day, and Mo went to bed early each evening.

He'd always loved the beach as a child. He bet Mo did, too. Suddenly he realized the last time he'd been to the beach had been several years ago, when he and Fatima had visited friends in Cannes. It had been shortly before she died. One day on the sand had been enough. Lying in the sun doing nothing had never been his idea of fun.

But he wouldn't just be lying around with his son. They'd swim and build sand castles. He bet Bridget had more ideas for a day at the beach.

"She's an interesting young woman," his grandmother said, sipping her chocolate. "Kind enough to spend some time with me reading that book and explaining the Americanisms."

"She enjoys it. So she says."

"She and her cousin are very unlike. I wasn't sure that first night," she said pensively.

"Very different," he agreed. "Don't worry about Saturday, everything will be fine. Just come to watch the match, do not worry about a thing."

"Enjoy your outing with Bridget," she said politely, her gaze thoughtful.

Rashid nodded and left. He was doing a kindness to a guest. She had expressed an interest in seeing some of the treasures of his country. If he visited San Francisco, he was sure she'd offer to show him around.

Anticipation rose. He looked forward to the day as he hadn't looked forward to something in a long time.

Rashid leaned against the car, checked his watch once more. It was still a minute before ten, the time he'd told her they'd leave. He wondered for a brief moment if she'd show up, or send some excuse. After that kiss, she'd fled the garden like she was in a race. Throughout the evening she'd avoided him as much as possible without causing comment. But he'd seen her gaze turn his way when she thought he wasn't watching. When he'd met her eyes, she quickly looked away.

For the second time since his guests had arrived, he wished them all gone. All but Bridget.

He'd caught her alone before she retired and told her he'd take her to see the sights today. She'd been flustered, her indecision clearly evident. She truly wanted to go. Even if she had to put up with him, or that was the message he read.

Had the kiss meant more to her than he intended?

Hell, he wasn't even sure what he had intended. It had been spontaneous, not preplanned. He wanted her. He'd kissed her. End of story.

Or was it? What about the thought of kissing her again that never left? What about the desire to whisk her away from the others, to spend time with her, to see what might develop.

Not the long-term love she so ardently believed in. But men and women could spend time together without a lifelong commitment.

The door opened and Bridget stepped out. She was wearing one of the new outfits she'd chosen, a sleeveless top in some kind of blue, with a sheer white shirt over it. The skirt was a swirl of colors, her feet shod in strappy sandals.

Her eyes lit up when she saw him.

"Oh, we're taking the convertible, how cool."

It was the car that brought her delight, he thought wryly, feeling firmly put in his place. It was not a comfortable sensation. Was he as spoiled by attention normally given him from women? The thought was unsettling.

"Unless you fear burning by the sun," he said, opening the passenger side door for her.

"I've slathered on a ton of sunscreen. I would love to ride with the top down!" she said coming quickly down the stairs.

Rashid promptly joined her in the car and started the engine. With one last look at the front of the villa, he drove down the drive-way, feeling like they were sneaking away, except, of course, for the black sedan which followed. His bodyguards would see they en-joyed their day safely. His other guests were taken care of. Francesca had already left. He was merely extending his duties as host to show a guest around his country. So why did it feel like freedom?

Bridget settled back in her seat and donned her sunglasses. She'd quickly pulled her hair back into a barrette, so it wouldn't become disheveled while they were driving. The wind against her face felt fabulous. She tilted her seat back, enjoying the freedom. She glanced at Rashid, amazed she had found the courage to come today.

She'd thought of nothing but him since his kiss. It had thrilled her to her toes, and worried her beyond end. She'd bid her cousin farewell, wishing she were staying longer so Bridget could discuss this turn of events. But Francesca had been longing to go.

There was no one else in the group she'd confide in. Maybe he had only been flirting, trying to cheer her up and she was reading too much into a single kiss.

Had her thank-you kiss on his cheek given him a false impression? She'd just been so happy she'd wanted to share that.

As recently as a week ago when her father died, she thought she'd never be happy again. But spending time here had shown her differently. She'd always miss her father, as she did her mother. But life did move on and she could find moments of sheer bliss if she looked for them.

Like riding in a convertible with the sexiest man she'd ever known. Could she get a picture to show her friends? Marcie would never believe it. And Sharon would be green with envy—in a happy way for Bridget. She wished they could meet Rashid.

''Where are we going?'' She would put the kiss behind her and enjoy the day. It wasn't likely it would be repeated.

''First we will tour the city. Many of our oldest buildings were designed by the French. There are some public gardens that are in bloom now, with landscaping that is constantly changing. Later, if you like, we can visit a monument on the edge of the desert dating from World War II when the Germans occupied our land for a while.''

"Rommel?"

"One of his contingencies."

"I've read about the North African campaign. Did he do much damage?"

"No, but our people did sufficient damage to him and his troops, that he quickly moved to vacate our territory."

"Tell me the history of your country. What is its primary industry, how many people live here? How is it you and your family speak such perfect English? Is that a second language here?"

"I attended school in England, from the age of seven. My father had before me. His father had gone to school in France," Rashid explained.

"Seven? You were sent away from home at age seven?" she interrupted. "I can't believe that. You would have been only two years older than Mo. You aren't thinking about sending him away are you?"

He glanced at her. Bridget couldn't imagine a little boy leaving all he knew to go to boarding school—not if his parents were around to take care of him.

"It is the custom."

"Mo's only a little boy. He needs his family around, especially after losing his mother so young. I'm sure you have schools here."

"Of course we do, but it's been the custom in my family for the sons to be educated abroad. Strengthens our ties with other countries and gives us a wider education."

"But the girls stay home?"

He nodded.

"Sexist," she muttered beneath her breath.

He smiled but wisely kept silent.

Bridget took a deep breath. She needn't get caught up in Mo's future. She was a one time guest. If their cultural ways were different from hers, she had to accept that. But her heart ached for little Mo. Maybe Rashid would send him to school in California. She could visit him then and have him visit her at home.

She shook her head. What was she think-ing? She'd enjoy her visit and return home. There would be no reason to keep in touch. Rashid was Francesca's friend. He had ex-tended her an invitation to visit only to help out Francesca's cousin.

"This part of the highway covers the old caravan trails. Merchants used to come from Spain to North Africa and then east on the spice trade. Alidan started as an oasis before it grew into our capital city. Fortunately, as it turned out, there is water enough to support millions. It was an important stopping point for the traders in the old days, now our most progressive city," Rashid began.

Bridget looked around, trying to forget about Mo and take in all she could.

The morning flew by as Rashid proved to be an entertaining and informative tour guide. The city was similar to other large cities, cars vying for space on the crowded streets, pe-destrians hurrying along the wide sidewalks. Street vendors sold their wares from kiosks along the major boulevards. The old buildings rose gleaming in the sunlight, dwarfing trees that had been planted along the road side. Elegant and fanciful, the buildings caught her imagination.

Some had inlaid tile, others relief work. Still others had a feel of old New Orleans, with iron balconies and railings. She was fascinated.

When they drove out into the desert a short distance, the countryside changed drastically. Quickly gone was any sign of habitation, only the rising sand dunes marched ahead of them to the horizon. It was hard to remember the large city only a few miles behind them.

"Water is so precious here, isn't it," she said, studying the desolate scene.

"Life giving and life sustaining." He drove into a small parking area. Before them stood abandoned ruins of what had once been a military compound. A lone scraggly tree gave scant shade against the noonday sun.

"This is where the final battle was fought between the Germans and our people. Seventy-three Aboul Sarians died. But many more Germans. Rommel felt it wasn't worth staying when he had more pressing needs with Montgomery on his flank.''

Bridget felt as if ghosts haunted the lonely outpost. She glanced around and was sad that their last sights had been of such a bleak place. Alidan was truly a lovely lush city. The contrast was amazing.

''Lunch?'' Rashid asked.

She blinked and nodded, still studying the lonely abandoned buildings. ''It won't be many more decades before it's totally gone,'' she mused. ''Swept away by the sand.''

''Storms waste away the walls. I'm surprised it's lasted this long. By the time Mo has children, I expect there to only be the marker.''

''Thank you for bringing me. For taking time to show me some of your country,'' she said. ''So far my favorite place was the City Gardens.''

''After seeing you at my estate, I figured they would be. There's a small café on the edge of the city where we can eat. If you like, afterward, we can head for the sea. It's not a long drive.''

''No, thank you. I'd rather go to the beach with Mo. Maybe we could borrow your driver and spend an afternoon there.''

She'd much rather go with Rashid, but she would be embarrassed if everyone knew of her avid interest in her host. She had to work at hiding her feelings. Keep it light.

''Maybe we should head back,'' she said slowly, knowing he had already spent far more time with her than his other guests. Yet she would cherish the memory of their day together. If only she still believed in fairy tales.

''After lunch. I think you will like the café. We can run by the club on the way home to see where we'll play polo on Saturday,'' Rashid said easily.

''I'd like that. How did you get involved in polo? Do you play often?'' She was curious for any information about him. Treasuring each fact, knowing she'd think about him often when she returned home.

Bridget was delighted that Rashid didn't press returning. He seemed to want to spend more time with her. Trying to feel comfortable in his presence, she was relieved he didn't regret his impulse to take her sightseeing. The others had visited before. Undoubtedly seeing all they wanted earlier, she was the only one interested today.

"My uncle plays. I remember going to matches to see him when I was small. When I was at school in England, I picked up the sport, and have been playing ever since. Jack urges me on, as you might have guessed," Rashid said.

She couldn't imagine anyone urging Rashid on to anything he didn't wish to do. He was the most self-sufficient, in command man she'd ever met.

"You have your own horse, then."

"I have a stable full. I usually change horses between each chukker—period of the match. Jack and Charles will borrow some of my mounts to use on Saturday since neither brought horses on this visit. I have a couple of favorites. When we play, I rotate the horses. They are constantly being trained.''

''You have trainers?'' She tried to visualize how big a venture this was.

''Of course. I also ride the horses in practice. Practice makes a good player, as well as keeps the horses in top form.''

''I'd love to see the horses sometime. I always wanted a horse when I was a child, but we lived in San Francisco. Sort of like living in downtown Alidan and wishing for a horse.''

''We'll go to the stables before we head for home. I have a mare ready to deliver soon. Maybe before you leave, you'll be able to see a new foal.''

''Oh, I'd love that! I used to beg my parents for a horse. My mother would never allow me to even entertain thoughts about one day having one. But on one visit to Italy, my grandfather offered to buy me one if I'd stay with them. My mother was horrified, but Papa just laughed and said he couldn't be apart from his little girl.'' Her voice broke on the last as she remembered that happy vacation, and the fact both her parents were now gone.

"Sounds like your grandfather was a troublemaker."

"No, he was just teasing, only I was too young to understand. I couldn't have left my parents." She looked at Rashid. "I was nine at the time. Imagine how awful it would be for Mo to leave at even a younger age."

"I don't have to imagine, I can remember," he said dryly.

"Oh, of course. I never thought about that. Were you lonely? Did you feel lost? You seem so self-sufficient, I have trouble remembering you were once a little boy."

"It wasn't all bad. I made friends. I learned a new language, and had a lot more freedom than I had had here. I came home for summers, to make sure I didn't lose my heritage," he explained.

"You could have stayed here for school and gone visiting summers," she countered.

He stopped at a roadside café a few moments later. When they walked into the patio behind the restaurant, Bridget was enchanted. High stone walls surrounded the flagstone area, a large fountain splashed in the center. There were few tables, affording a measure of privacy to all. They were seated at one near a corner of the wall. Deep purple bougainvillea flourished as a background.

''For a desert country, there are tons of flowers,'' she commented gazing around.

''Water makes the difference. When we have it, we use it. Where we don't, you see the sand.''

Bridget opened her menu and promptly closed it. ''You'll have to order for me, this is in Arabic.''

''What would you like?''

''Something with fruit, please.''

A few moments later, their order taken, and a pot of hot tea set on the table, Rashid looked at her.

''About that kiss,'' he said.

Bridget met his gaze, startled he'd brought it up. She'd done her best to ignore her reactions, to keep a distance last night between them.

"It never should have happened. You're Francesca's friend," she said quickly.

"That's all we are, Bridget, friends. You and I are friends as well, aren't we?" he countered.

"Not close friends."

"Maybe I want to change that."

She hesitated, unsure what was going on. What was Rashid playing at? She was visiting for a few days, then would return to her normal life. She and a sheikh had nothing in common.

"Change it how?" she asked warily.

"Get to know each other, spend some time together while you are visiting." He reached out and took her hand in his, holding firmly when she tried to tug free. "You are on vacation, enjoy yourself while you're here. Let's explore where this attraction takes us."

"That's typical of a man," she complained, pulling harder until he released her.

"What is?"

"Enjoy the moment, then move on to the next one."

"Enjoying the moment is not a good thing?"

"Okay, that's not exactly what I meant. Enjoy the person of the moment, I should have said. Have a vacation fling, isn't that what you're suggesting?"

He said nothing and she felt a wave of embarrassment sweep through her. Heat warmed her cheeks and she knew they'd be bright pink.

"I'm sorry, I thought that's what you were saying," she muttered, wishing she could sink beneath the table.

"I was not offering an affair, only friendship," he said formally. Leaning back, he surveyed the courtyard. Several tables were empty, the others occupied by couples or groups intent on themselves. No one was paying any attention to them.

She'd insulted him. "I'm sorry, Rashid. I misunderstood. I would be honored to be counted as a friend of yours."

He met her gaze and nodded once.

Bridget had known she was out of her league. A kiss meant nothing to most people, a momentary expression of fun, or delight, or affection. A sharing of a special moment. Not a lifelong commitment.

Rashid was a worldly sheikh, a man used to jetting to London or Paris or Cairo at a moment's notice, and smoothly fitting in wherever he went. He was used to sophisticated women—like Francesca and Marie and Elizabeth. Not shy librarians who saw things that weren't there.

She hoped she hadn't ruined their day with her wild thoughts. Was it because she longed so much for another kiss, for another compliment? He had told her beautiful cousin that she, Bridget Rossi, was lovely. She would cling to that thought and try to match her actions to his, not become suspicious and see things that weren't there, no matter how much she might wish they were.

By the time the luncheon was served, Bridget had her emotions under control. Gradually she opened up again, and tried to maintain a friendly attitude, even with every cell in her body attuned to Rashid, every inch of her longing for a closer touch. She should have let him hold her hand. She should have seen if he'd kiss her again.

She should have her head examined if she thought Rashid thought of her in that way!

After lunch, Rashid stopped at a small shop and bought Bridget a pair of sturdy shoes to wear at the stable.

"I told you I could wear a pair I already had," she said, when he tossed her the package.

"And I said they'd get ruined. You need substantial shoes for walking in the muck."

"I'll pay you back when we get home."

"Bridget, I can afford a new pair of shoes, don't be ridiculous."

"You shouldn't be buying me anything. I'm the one who wants to see the stable."

"Are you always so argumentative?" he asked as they sped toward home.

"Only when I know I'm right."

"Take the blasted shoes or I won't let you see my horses."

She laughed. "Gosh, what a threat. If we don't play nicely, you'll take your toys and go home."

He looked at her and the light in his eyes had her heart speeding up. If they hadn't been going down the highway at a hundred kilometers an hour, she knew he would have kissed her to stop the argument. It was all she could do to stay on her side of the car. She longed to lean against him, snuggle up and find out what might result from two *friends* becoming closer. She had never wanted anything as much in her life.

Prudence kept her on her side of the car.

The stables were huge and in pristine condition. Bridget saw Jack riding a horse in one arena to the right. In a corral adjacent to the stable three horses ran along the fence, as if trying to keep pace with Jack and his mount.

Rashid came around the car to let her out, and gestured to the horses running. ''They are some of my new stock, trying to keep up. The mare I told you about is inside. We are keeping her segregated as her time approaches.''

They walked into the stable, and while it was clean, there were still puddles, wet straw and the distinctive aroma of horse. But no muck in this pristine stable.

Bridget loved it all, including the Arabian mare who put her head over the stall door and nickered softly when Rashid approached.

''Oh, she's so beautiful,'' she exclaimed.

Rashid took her hand to hold up near the mare. She blew softly against Bridget's palm, then nudged it. He released her to pet the horse. She was charmed.

''She likes me,'' she said in delight. Her brief riding forays had been long ago. How wonderful it must be to have horses available at any time.

"She's pampered, and ready to deliver, aren't you Asheera," Rashid said, running his hand over her sleek neck.

"That's her name, Asheera?"

"Yes. This is her first foal, so we are watching her closely." He nodded to cameras mounted high above the stall. "Someone monitors her constantly. When it's time, we'll be there to assist if needed."

"Is she one of the polo horses?"

"She has been trained, but usually I prefer a bigger mount. Most of my polo horses are Thoroughbreds. Come, you can meet Halsin, another favorite."

With a last rub on Asheera's velvety nose, Bridget followed.

Rashid whistled sharply when they went to the other side of the barn and a magnificent black horse rushed to the stall door. He was larger than Asheera, glowing with health and vitality. He tossed his head and pawed the ground, then hung his head over the stall door to nuzzle Rashid.

"He's the first one I will ride on Saturday."

"Wow, I bet he's a handful." And she knew Rashid could master him with no difficulty.

Rashid showed her two more horses. As they were leaving the stable, a pony stuck his head over a shallow door.

"Oh, Mo's pony, no doubt," she said, moving to see him. He was a dapple-gray.

"Yes, he learned to ride last year. Sometimes we ride together."

"Not playing polo, I hope," she said, in dismay.

"You are very protective of my son, Bridget. Do you not think I take care of him?"

"Yes, of course you do. I don't know much about children beyond what I see at the library, but he seems so small, and you, um, have other obligations. Wasn't four young to learn to ride?"

"He never rides unattended. You don't believe I spend as much time with him as I should?" Rashid's tone was silky.

"I would never presume to tell you how much time you should spend with your son," she said. "But if it was me, I'd spend lots of time with him. He's such a darling child and children grow up so fast."

"Next week we'll all go to the beach," Rashid said, taking her hand and starting toward the car. "Even Mo."

"I'll look forward to it. Thank you for today. I've had such a good time."

"It was my pleasure."

He stopped by the car but made no move to open the door, turning he looked at Bridget.

"We are friends, and sometimes friends exchange kisses." With that, he leaned over and kissed her.

Bridget couldn't move. She could only feel, savoring the touch of his mouth, the gentle persuasion as his lips moved against hers. When she opened her mouth, he deepened the kiss and wrapped his arms tightly around her.

She leaned into the kiss, reveling in the sensations that spread through every cell.

His embrace was intoxicating. She forgot her sadness, her concerns for the future, everything, swept away to a magical place where Rashid was her only reality. Time seemed to spin out of control as the kiss went on endlessly. She never wanted it to stop.

But end it did, slowly, as if Rashid were as reluctant as she to stop.

She opened her eyes and found his dark ones waiting.

''No regrets,'' he said.

She shook her head. Never a regret. She wanted more. But conscious of where they were, she summoned a smile and stepped back until she touched the car.

''I will treasure today,'' she said, turning to get in before she did something else foolish, like insist he kiss her again.

CHAPTER SIX

BRIDGET felt decidedly awkward when she sat down to dinner that evening. She knew better than to talk herself into believing Rashid wanted to be friends. A playboy's idea of friendship differed from hers. He'd been kind to show her around. How many people did she know who could boast having been kissed by a sheikh? She would treasure his kisses as a precious memory.

But once back in San Francisco, she'd get back in the routine of her normal life and the brief vacation in the Mediterranean would be tucked away.

Watching him throughout dinner, she didn't see any evidence that he paid special attention to any of his guests. It reaffirmed her belief he'd merely been kind.

No one had even hinted at more.

And she would not let herself fantasize about a long-term relationship. She wanted to be married one day. To have a husband to adore her. To have children to lavish her love upon.

Rashid had been married, and Bridget knew firsthand how second wives fared. It was not for her.

Salina al Besoud summoned her when they adjourned to the drawing room after dinner.

"How was your tour of the city?" she asked Bridget once they were seated at a sofa with a huge silver coffeepot on the table before them.

"It was lovely. I learned quite a bit about your country's history while Rashid kindly showed me around. Some of the buildings in the old part of the city are quite fabulous. I would have loved to have gone inside to see if the decor matched the elegance of the facades."

"Another time, perhaps. I'm glad you went with him. He loves our country. No one else seems interested in such pursuits."

"I love history and exploring new places. I would like to go back and spend more time. Or see a different part of the country," Bridget said.

"It can be arranged. Ask Rashid."

Bridget smiled politely and nodded, knowing she would never ask. She'd treasure today's memory for what it was, a host making sure a guest enjoyed herself.

Laughter rang out from the group near the French doors. Bridget looked over at the same moment Rashid's gaze moved to her. For a second she felt her heart catch, then begin to beat rapidly. She couldn't drag her eyes away. His eyes were alight, his smile warm and contagious. What had amused him? She had never heard him laugh before. The richness in the tone brought a smile to her face. Could she ever say anything to make him laugh so?

A moment later he excused himself, glancing around to make sure his guests were occupied. He walked over to Bridget and his grandmother.

''I hope you don't mind, Grandmother, but I am going to steal your companion away.''

''To where?'' she replied, studying him with some interest.

''Bridget has not yet seen the gardens at night. I thought she would enjoy it. Rain is expected soon, so this may be our last chance for a couple of evenings.''

He held out his hand and Bridget automatically placed hers in it. When he tightened his grip to assist her to rise, she felt as if a live current had jolted through her. She came to her feet quickly and tugged to free her hand.

His eyes told her he knew she had been affected by his touch, but he made no comment, merely motioning her toward the French doors. ''Shall we?''

''I should like to see the gardens at night, but won't you be missed?'' She put her hands behind her lest she give way to temptation to reach out and touch him.

He shrugged, ''My other guests seem occupied. It is not as if I'm the sole entertainment available. We won't be gone for long.''

Stepping outside, Bridget was buffeted by a strong breeze. ''The forerunner of the storm?'' she asked, brushing a strand of hair from her eyes. It felt fresh. She felt exhilarated.

''We will have rain before the night is over. A thunderstorm is predicted, with rain to follow all tomorrow. Come, as you can see, our way is lighted.''

Small lamps softly illuminated the paths. Placed several feet apart, the dim lighting was enough to enable her to clearly see where they were walking. Certain bushes and statues had been highlighted with a spotlight, giving a dramatic flare to the garden.

''It's lovely,'' she murmured, following another spotlight which rested on a rose bush in full bloom. ''It's as if certain plants were singled out for special notice while they might blend in with the rest during the day.''

''The gardeners change the spots as different bushes come into bloom,'' he said. ''We can have a different walk each evening of the week with the mere changing of the lamps.''

"You are fortunate to have such a lovely estate," she said, delighting in the effects of the lighting. It made the entire garden seem like a fairy-tale setting. The breeze caused the bushes and vines to dance beneath its onslaught, but the refreshing air kicked every sense into full awareness. Including her closeness to Rashid.

"I have pots of plants on my balcony, which are a poor substitute. I inherited my father's home, so I can have a garden again if I move back. It would never compare with this, but I like the idea of movable spotlights. I might try that at home," she said as they ambled along.

"Is your home large?"

"Bigger than I'll need alone. But I hope to marry one day, and it will be perfect for a family."

"Ah, the man whom you can envision being with in fifteen and thirty years," he said.

"Exactly."

The wind gusted and blew another strand in her face. Rashid reached out and brushed it back, tucking it behind her ear. It felt as if his fingers lingered.

"Whomever you marry will be a lucky man," he said softly.

Her heart warmed. "What a lovely thing to say!" Bridget couldn't remember anyone ever saying they'd be lucky to know her, much less be married to her.

As they rounded the bend, there was only the lighting on the path, nothing was highlighted. The wind seemed to grow stronger, the stars were now completely obliterated by storm clouds.

Bridget felt wound up. She knew some of the feeling was due to the weather, but most of it was due to Rashid. She turned to tell him how much she was enjoying her visit. Before she could say a word, however, he reached out to cradle her head in his hands, leaning closer.

"You intrigue me, Bridget Rossi," he said before he kissed her.

Bridget's sense of adventure went into high gear as she stepped into his embrace.

Her own arms encircled his neck, tightening as she pressed herself against him, reveling in the sensations that swept through her. The wind blotted out background noise. The darkness was complete with her eyes shut, the pounding of her heart filled every cell, beating faster and faster.

Thunder rumbled in the distance—or was it her blood pounding a drumbeat? Light strobed behind her lids, or was it lightning shattering the darkness?

Wrapped in Rashid's arms, she felt as if she was sheltered from all of life's harms.

A man hurried around the curve in the path, speaking urgently. Rashid raised his head and uttered a harsh comment in Arabic. The man did not retreat, however, but stood his ground, speaking rapidly.

''Damn.'' Rashid released Bridget. ''There are few things that could end this, but my mare is about to deliver. We do not anticipate any problems, but this is her first and it is wise to watch closely.'' He snapped out orders to the man who then turned and disappeared.

"I'll escort you back to the drawing room," Rashid said, turning back toward the house.

"Can I come? I should love to see a baby horse born," Bridget said, loath to end her time with Rashid.

He looked at her clothes and seemed to be weighing his decision.

"You would have to change. It can get messy. Wear your oldest clothes. I'll stop by your room in a few minutes. We'll take a car to the stables, the rain won't be far off."

"Will we be in time?" she asked as they hurried along the path. The beauty of the garden was forgotten as she tried to decide what she could wear. Nothing she had with her was old, especially not the pants she'd just bought. The navy pair she'd tucked in at the last moment when packing for Italy would have to do. She just hoped they wouldn't be utterly ruined.

"It could be hours before the birth. However, the storm is frightening Asheera. Perhaps I can calm her," he said, lengthening his stride.

Rashid bypassed the drawing room, leading Bridget directly to the stairs. He did not wish to have Jack and Charles tagging along. He knew they would both be interested, but this time he wanted only Bridget.

He changed into old clothes before heading back to her bedroom. Fatima had never cared much about his horses, though she rode from time to time. He rarely even talked about them with the other women he'd dated over the years since her death. Bridget was the first to show interest beyond admiring them when on the game field.

He knocked on her door.

"Be there in a sec," she called.

He checked his watch just as she opened her door. Amazed, he gazed at her. He knew of no other woman who could have been ready so quickly.

Bridget wore a dark pullover and navy pants. The sturdy shoes he'd bought were the only thing really suitable, but he knew no one had suggested she bring old clothes suitable for foaling. The navy pants and top would have to do.

''I'm ready,'' she said breathlessly. Her cheeks were flushed, her eyes sparkled. She looked as if she'd been made love to. He wished for a moment Asheera had chosen another night to foal.

''Come, a car should be waiting.''

In only moments they were at the stable. The lights had been turned down low, to provide a more soothing atmosphere for the nervous mare. The grooms stood nearby, ready to lend assistance if necessary, but leaving the mare alone for the time being.

Walking to the stall, Rashid mentally ran through all the problems that could occur. He'd asked one of the grooms to summon the vet. Nothing else could be done unless there were complications. It was all up to Asheera.

The mare was fretful, stomping in the stall, whinnying when the thunder rolled. Her nervousness was obvious.

He spoke to her in his native tongue, softly, cajolingly. He wanted this birth to go smoothly. He knew she would deliver fine offspring, especially with the stallion he'd bred with her. It was unfortunate she chose such a stormy night, but it couldn't be stopped now.

The sound of his voice calmed her slightly, but once the thunder rolled again, she grew agitated.

The rain came with a rush, pounding on the roof. She neighed long and loud. An answering sound came from another of the stalls. The stormfront moved in, pouring rain, flashing lightning and rumbling continuously. Rashid calmly soothed the fretful mare, Bridget leaning over the door, watching them. Gradually the storm moved through and the thunder diminished, soon fading completely. The background sound of the rain at last seemed to calm Asheera and soon she was standing docily beside Rashid. He ran his hands along her neck, down her side, feeling the belly harden as a contraction took hold. The foal would be born before dawn he estimated.

"You're doing well, my friend," he said soothingly, glad the worst seemed past.

Bridget hadn't said a word since he entered the stall.

"She'll be all right, I think," he said in English, stepping back and heading to the door. Slipping out into the walkway, he shut it firmly, leaning on the top to watch Asheera.

"So it's like with a human, then, several hours of labor?" she asked.

"Yes. Often the first one takes the longest."

The mare walked to the door and leaned her head over, snuffling against his shoulder. He stroked her neck. "She wants company. I'll have one of the grooms put some bales of hay in her stall. Chairs might prove dangerous to her if she becomes agitated again. Are you comfortable sitting in there with her?

I think she'll remain calm now that the worst of the storm has passed.''

Bridget nodded, feeling apprehensive, but not willing to ever let Rashid know that. He would not have suggested it if it were dangerous.

Rashid gave the orders. The stable was cozy with its smell of hay and horses, the dim lights and the soft sound of rain on the roof.

A few moments later they sat side by side on a bale of hay watching Asheera drift around in her spacious stall.

''You've probably seen a lot of births,'' Bridget said once settled.

''Not that many. My first was when I was just a year older than Mo. Then I went away to school and didn't see another until I was in my twenties. It never grows old.''

''I expect it's like a miracle each time,'' she said.

He nodded, pleased she felt the same way he always felt. Maybe next time Mo would be old enough to attend.

Time passed slowly. The grooms lingered nearby, to be ready for any order he might have. The vet arrived, examined Asheera and declared everything in order. He went to the tack room to get some coffee to pass the time until he was needed.

Rashid looked at Bridget. She had leaned back against the stall wall and her eyes were almost closed.

''You should return to the house, get some rest,'' he said softly. They'd had a long day, and it was approaching dawn. She'd been up far too long.

''No, I want to be here. But waiting's hard. I'm tired. Why don't you talk to me so I stay awake?'' she said, rolling her head toward him and opening her eyes slightly.

He felt a tightening in his gut when she looked at him like that. Sleepy, sexy.

He wanted her.

If Asheera wasn't about to foal, he'd take her in a dark stall and kiss her. Or order the car to return them to the villa where they could be alone in one of the bedrooms, for what remained of the night. Conscious of the men who were nearby, he quelled his desire—for the moment.

''And what shall we talk about?'' How I would love to kiss that bridge of freckles across your nose? How I would love to tangle my hands in your silky hair and run the strands through my fingers? How I would love to hear you catch your breath as you do just before my lips claim yours?

''Did your wife share your love of horses?'' she asked.

He looked away in frustration. He wanted her, she wanted to talk about Fatima. Or was it merely a ploy to change the subject? He glanced at her again, but she was studying the mare.

''Fatima didn't care for horses. The gardens were her delight. She was an indifferent rider, and only went when we had company who wished to ride.''

''But Mo likes them.''

''Of course.'' Rashid couldn't imagine having a son who didn't share his love of horses.

"If you marry again, do you plan to seek a woman to share your love of horses?" she asked lazily, her head still resting against the wall.

"Not necessarily. Her functions would be different."

"Her functions?"

"Her role in my life, should I say."

"Sheesh, you sound like you'll be hiring an assistant or something."

"Aren't spouses assistants to each other? I would want a woman who could play hostess to my friends when I invite them to visit, to deal with the social aspects of my business, to be comfortable talking with ambassadors and presidents as she would be dealing with my family."

"Someone your parents arrange for you to marry, of course," she said.

He thought about that. Fatima had impressed him as being the perfect mate, sophisticated, cosmopolitan and beautiful. His parents had chosen her. Their life together had been pleasant.

But now he had doubts. Did he want the same thing if he married again? He slid a glance to Bridget. Her eyes were shut. Her hair had been hastily tied back to keep it out of her face. She looked tired. And so lovely he ached with wanting her.

''They arranged my first marriage. I plan to arrange my next on my own—if I marry again.''

''Would you pick someone like Fatima? You had a common background, but did you share any interests in common?''

''Mo.''

She opened her eyes and smiled. He felt his heart kick into high gear. She had the most enchanting smile, probably because of the way it lit up her eyes.

''He would be a common enough interest. Do you want lots more kids?'' she asked.

''Lots more?'' he shook his head. ''Maybe one or two.''

''Mmm. I want maybe half a dozen. And dogs and cats and bunnies. I want to give my kids the most perfect childhood so they'll have a strong basis in life when they are out on their own.''

''Your own life seems to have a strong basis,'' he said.

Bridget shrugged. ''My father didn't love my mother and I knew it. I know he loved me, don't get me wrong. And I think he had some affection for Mum. But nothing like his passion for his beautiful Isabella.''

''That's a western view, that marriage must encompass wild passionate love,'' he scoffed gently. He'd heard this before.

Rashid thought about his cousin Yasmin. She had married for love, and seemed deliriously happy. She was the only one in the family he knew who openly displayed her affection for her husband and children wherever they were. His own mother and father were more formal with each other in public. Were they as formal in private?

Remembering how little Fatima and he had to talk about when alone, he suspected they were. Shared interests would have given them more to discuss when alone with each other than the last party they'd attended, or Mo's antics once he'd been born. Still, he had developed love for his wife. He missed her. And he mourned that Mo would not remember the gentle woman who had borne him.

Asheera gave a whinny. Rashid rose and went to the mare, rubbing her neck, speaking soothingly to her. She seemed more agitated. The vet came to the stall door, a cup of coffee in hand. He looked over at the mare.

''Won't be long, I'd say. Maybe your friend should come on this side of the partition.'' His English was heavily accented.

Rashid nodded and looked at Bridget. ''You should go out now. She's getting close and too many strangers will just make her more nervous.''

Bridget stood slowly and went to stand on the outside of the stall door as the vet changed places and entered. He finished his coffee, looked around and then handed her the empty cup. She leaned against the stall door and watched the proceedings, fascinated.

Despite being tired and undoubtably a bit uncomfortable, she was staying. He was glad.

Time seemed to move quickly as the mare prepared for the final stages of delivery. The foal arrived in a textbook perfect birth, feet-first, the sack breaking before he was fully delivered.

Rashid glanced at Bridget, struck by the sheer delight on her face. Her eyes shimmered with tears, her smile was wide and honest. She truly was moved by the event.

"He's perfect," she whispered.

The vet checked both the mare and the foal, then stepped back to let nature take its course. The mare nuzzled her newborn, licking, caressing. In a short time the little foal struggled to rise onto his feet. Twice he collapsed, to the giggles of Bridget. Rashid smiled at the sight. Newborns were so awkward. Yet in less than a year, this foal would be a colt, running in the fields, growing into the strong Arabian stallion that would bring a hefty price when sold.

"Oh, Rashid, that was the most amazing thing." She laughed when the creature fell again. "Oh, poor thing, can't you help him up?"

"He'll manage, and be stronger for doing it himself," Rashid said, moving to stand near her as they watched. Soon the foal was on his feet, looking around as if to say, what next? His mother nuzzled him again, showing him where to nurse.

Rashid spoke to the vet and then to the grooms in Arabic. Turning to Bridget, Rashid let himself out of the stall. "They will watch to make sure nothing unforeseen happens and let me know if anything unexpected arises, otherwise, the excitement is over for tonight."

"Thank you for letting me be a part of it. Do you have a name picked out for him?" she asked.

"Not yet. We waited to see the sex. But we'll look at his bloodlines and see what name seems suitable. Come, it's almost morning, you must be exhausted."

It was still drizzling when they left the stable, hurrying for the car that waited. In no time they were back at the villa, and climbing the stairs inside the quiet house. The rest of the guests would be rising soon, but Rashid urged Bridget to sleep as late as she liked.

"It'll rain all day. I'll organize some activities for those who need to be entertained, so don't get up until you feel like it," he said when they reached the top of the stairs.

"I'm reading to Mo in the afternoon. I think he'll be ready for that if he can't go outside because of the weather," she said sleepily.

Rashid took her arms in his hands, holding her in front of him. "I've said it before, you are not here to entertain my son."

"It truly is my pleasure. Mo asks for so little. He's a darling little boy, and smart—you must be so proud of him."

Rashid thought about the son he hardly knew. He suspected Bridget had learned more about Mo's likes and dislikes in the short time she'd been here than he knew.

Fatima had been in charge of the household and their child.

"Come join us, if you wish," she said shyly.

He'd rather join her in her bedroom now, shut the door behind them and slowly make love to her. He'd open the windows and let the rain-cooled air flow over them to contrast with the heat they'd generate, then to cool them down for sleep. He'd delight in learning what she liked and what brought her pleasure. Share pillow talk that would bind her closer and make her forget for a time her nebulous dream of a loving husband. He wanted her attention entirely, not to share it with some dream.

But she was a guest in his household. She was young, innocent and nothing like the women he usually slept with. She could be hurt, and for some reason, he didn't want to be the person to cause any hurt to her.

"Sleep well—maybe I will join you and Mo this afternoon." He kissed her, holding on to his control lest the kiss get out of hand and he forgot his principles and swept her into bed.

CHAPTER SEVEN

WHEN Bridget reached her room, her heart still pounded. She was warmed through and through and cracked the window open a bit to let in the cool air before changing to slip beneath the covers. She was tired, yet buoyed beyond anything. What a miracle the birth had been. She'd wanted to hug the mare, hug the baby, hug Rashid. She had never seen anything like it. If she lived here, she'd attend every birth on the place!

Of course, that would never happen. Their discussion about marriage once again pointed out the vast differences in their views and beliefs. Rashid had married to please his parents, then fallen in love with his wife. He saw no need to change that process. But what if he married again and didn't fall in love with his wife?

Bridget was a product of a loveless marriage. She was holding out for something vastly different. Not for her the mistakes of her parents. Or some arranged marriage that might or might not work out.

She wanted to be swept away with love. To know the man she gave her heart to would love her to the end of time. She would be special to him, like her papa's beloved Isabella had been.

But just before falling asleep she let her imagination envision Rashid madly in love with her, and she with him. Without thought, she envisioned him in fifteen years, twenty, thirty. She had no trouble imagining a happy life that would suit her forever if he only loved her.

When she woke, it was almost noon. Hurrying to shower and dress, she joined the others in the dining room just as lunch was served at one. Her gaze went immediately to Rashid. He looked as rested and fit as ever. Had he slept at all, or had the duties of host prevented that?

"So I heard you saw the foal born," Jack said when the meal had been served.

"I did. It was fantastic," Bridget said, smiling in remembrance.

"All foals are born in the middle of the night," Salina al Besoud said.

"It seems that way, but I do think some are born in daylight," Rashid said.

Elizabeth and Marie began to talk about going shopping since the rain continued. Bridget didn't need to go, she had more than enough from her earlier shopping expedition.

"Do you wish to join them?" Rashid asked.

Bridget shook her head. "I have plans to read a book to a certain young man. A rainy afternoon is perfect for that."

When lunch was finished, Elizabeth caught up with Bridget as they walked back to their rooms.

"If you think playing up to Rashid's family is going to change anything, forget it. You are not in the running for second wife. He will be guided by his parents in that matter.

So no matter how much you try to ingratiate yourself by reading to his grandmother and baby-sitting his son, you will not win,'' she said.

Bridget blinked, stunned by the woman's assessment. ''I'm not trying to play up to anything. I enjoy spending time with his son. I'm only here on a visit. I'll be leaving soon.''

''Just didn't want you to get any ideas,'' she said. ''He's been a widower for several years now, and I don't see that changing, no matter how much women flirt with him.''

Bridget shrugged. ''I have it on absolute authority I'm not his type.'' Bridget had no intention of mentioning his kisses. But until he was committed to another relationship, he was free to bestow them where he would. They were hurting no one. As long as she could keep in mind that once she left, he'd turn his attentions elsewhere. She had to remember that or risk heartbreak.

Elizabeth seemed surprised. ''What type is his?''

''He wants someone who is comfortable speaking with ambassadors, being the perfect hostess and looking beautiful. You and Marie sound as if you're accustomed to his kind of life. I'm not. He's merely being kind to me while I'm here.''

''Well, I have to say staying up all night in a smelly barn isn't my idea of romance,'' Elizabeth said with a sniff.

''His wife Fatima never attended a birth,'' Bridget offered. She thought it sad that he and his wife had had so little in common. Maybe he would be happy with a trophy bride, but she wished more for him, as she did for herself.

''If you aren't trying to score off points, why do you want to tie yourself up with some old woman who hasn't been doing anything exciting for about fifty years?''

''His grandmother had an American mystery which is entertaining for both of us. I'm not sure what your motives are, Elizabeth, but I'm not getting my hopes up or looking for more of a relationship than exists right now. I'm a guest in Rashid's home, that all.''

''No motives beyond giving you a word of advice,'' Elizabeth said. She tossed her head and took off toward her room.

Bridget watched, wondering if that had been the woman's only motive. Could it be she was so dissatisfied with her own relationship with Charles, she was looking to spread the unhappiness? No matter. Bridget didn't need warnings. She could look after herself.

Rashid checked his watch as he walked toward the playroom. It had taken longer than he had expected to bundle two women into a car and send them on a shopping expedition. He had to give directions to the driver for the different shops they wanted to visit.

Then he had to set Jack and Charles up in the billiards room.

Finally his time was his own.

Opening the door, he faced a white missile headed his way. Snatching the paper airplane from the air before it could hit his face, he looked at Mo.

His son was laughing so hard he could scarcely stand. In Arabic he said, "You caught it, Papa. I would have gone farthest if you hadn't. It doesn't count."

"In English, please, Mo. Our guest doesn't understand," Rashid said, stepping into the room.

Bridget scrambled up from her place on the floor and grinned. "I don't understand the language, but I know interference when I see it. Was he calling foul?"

"He said I stopped him from winning."

She put her fists on her hips and shook her head. "Oh, no, you don't Mo. I would have won."

"Do it again. We have to do it again," the little boy said with relish.

Rashid handed Mo the paper airplane and shut the door behind him. "What did I interrupt?"

Mo rushed over to stand beside her, fairly dancing with anticipation.

''We are seeing who can send their airplane the farthest. Bridget wins more than me, but I won a few times,'' he explained.

''Have won,'' she corrected gently. ''And you sure have. Did you need something?'' she asked Rashid.

''Not at all. I came to see what you two were up to on a rainy afternoon.''

''Bridget is playing with me before going to see Grandmother. Then they will read a book and I shall color a picture for her to take home. She lives in America, you know. And if she has a picture I drawed, she will always remember me. Can she come back to visit?''

''I would be delighted to have her return for a visit,'' Rashid said. ''We need to make sure she enjoys this one so she will want to come again.'' He met her eyes over his son's head. He wanted to reach across the distance and draw her close.

''We are having fun,'' Mo stated firmly. ''She will want to come again.''

"Yes, I shall wish to. Maybe your father can judge our planes," she suggested, turning her attention on his son. Rashid felt a twinge of jealousy—of his little boy. He wanted her attention on him.

The afternoon passed swiftly. Mo was delighted to have two adults playing with him. After flying paper airplanes lost its appeal, they played two board games, neither familiar to Bridget, so Mo and Rashid had to explain the rules, and constantly offered her strategic suggestions. Mo won both and was pleased as punch.

Then Bridget suggested a game she sometimes used at children's hour at the library. They had moved to the comfortable sofa beneath one set of windows.

"I'll tell you a situation, and you tell me what you would do," she said.

"Okay," Mo said, sitting beside her and snuggling closer. Rashid sat beside his son, stretching his hand out along the back of the sofa. He almost touched Bridget's hair. He knew how soft it felt, would she notice if he rubbed a strand between his fingers?

"Okay, there's a huge dragon coming down the road. Fierce and breathing fire. What would you do?"

"That's easy," Mo said. "I'd give him a peanut butter and honey sandwich. Everybody loves those and he'd be so happy he wouldn't blow fire no more."

Rashid listened to his son's reply. "Peanut butter and honey? When have you ever had that?"

"Bridget says everyone loves peanut butter and honey sandwiches and it always makes her happy to eat one," Mo said.

She smiled wryly. "Comfort food, you know."

"Ah, and what else is comfort food for you?" Rashid asked.

"Pretty much anything chocolate. Now Mo, you have to make up a situation and ask your father what he would do," Bridget replied.

"Okay." He thought for a few moments, his face scrunched up in concentration. Rashid watched him, glancing once at Bridget to share his amusement at his son's determination. Her answering smile warmed him. It was the first time since Fatima died he felt connected with someone who shared his interest in and love of his son.

With a sudden realization, he knew Bridget loved Mo. She had an open, loving manner that couldn't fail to appeal to a small child who had lost his mother. Heck, it appealed to him, and his mother was still very much alive.

"What if we were at the beach and a giant wave came that would cover the beach and all of us. What would you do?" Mo asked seriously.

"I'd snatch you up, and dive through the wave to the other side where the sea would be calm and safe again," Rashid answered promptly.

"I can swim. I can hold my breath a long time," Mo said solemnly.

''Then we would have no problems getting to the other side of the giant wave. Do you want to take my turn to ask Bridget?''

''Okay. What if Papa showed up with lots of guests and you didn't know they were coming. What would you do?''

Bridget glanced at Rashid. ''Is that common?''

He shrugged. ''I usually give some notice to the staff.''

She looked at Mo. ''I would make a big pot of spaghetti and then a salad and make garlic bread. That would feed a crowd and when we were done, I'd take your father aside and scold him for not telling me earlier.''

Mo giggled. ''No one scolds Papa,'' he said.

''Maybe they should from time to time,'' she replied, throwing a saucy grin at Rashid.

''Or maybe I'm perfect just the way I am,'' Rashid teased.

''Or spoiled,'' she retorted quickly.

You could spoil me, Rashid thought. Her eyes were sparkling, her cheeks flushed with color. Her ready laughter captivated him. For an instant, he wished Mo wasn't with them. He'd draw her into his arms and kiss her until she didn't know her own name, or he didn't know his.

Before that line of fantasy took hold, he dragged his gaze from hers, focusing on Mo.

"Is that answer satisfactory?" he asked.

"Wouldn't she just tell cook?"

"Not if it was at my house. I do the cooking," Bridget said.

"You do?" Mo's eyes grew wide. "All by yourself?"

"Sure. And the cleaning, and laundry and everything. Not everyone has a staff at their beck and call."

Mo looked at his father for confirmation. Rashid felt a wave of love for his young son. He was still so trusting, relying on him for the truth. Would he grow to become cynical and distrusting? Would life be kind or harsh to his son? Rashid had an overwhelming yearning for Mo to stay as happy as he was this afternoon.

The immensity of his responsibility reared its head for the first time. Rashid had never fully realized the magnitude of the task ahead. For the first time in years, he achingly missed Fatima.

''Here's one for you, Mo,'' Bridget said. ''I'm due to read to your grandmother and I'm late. She was expecting me at three.''

''I'd run really fast,'' Mo said.

''Or you will get scolded,'' Rashid said, rising. ''Mo, would you like to come see Asheera's new foal?''

''Yes!'' He jumped up and hurried to the door.

''Go tell Alaya where you will be, and get a jacket, it's cool out with the rain,'' Rashid instructed.

Mo ran into the adjoining room.

''Thank you, Bridget Rossi, for bringing such happiness into the life of my son,'' Rashid said, taking her hand in his and bringing it to his mouth. He kissed her palm gently, smelling the sweet scent. Holding her gaze with his, he hoped she could see he wanted more. A brief affair until she had to leave. Would she be willing?

They could continue later in San Francisco. He could visit her, have her make him spaghetti and garlic bread and a peanut butter and honey sandwich. He wanted to see where she lived. To see her at work, to watch her captivate children at her reading hour. None could be more captivated than his son.

"I have to go, I really am late. I hope your grandmother won't be upset," she said, slowly pulling her hand from his.

"Tell her where you were, she dotes on Mo, so I think she'll forgive you."

Bridget closed her fingers over her palm, as if she could hold his kiss forever. She headed for the door, hoping he couldn't tell her knees felt as weak as soggy noodles. Hurrying down the corridor a moment later, she tried to remind herself it had been nothing but a thank-you kiss from a grateful father for her spending time with his son.

But it didn't feel like a grateful father's kiss. It felt wonderful. Daring. Romantic.

"Nonsense," she said aloud.

Knocking on the sitting room door a few moments later, she entered when bade to do so.

"I'm sorry for being late, Madame," she said to the woman sitting on a love seat. "I was with Mo and quite let the time slip by."

"Reading to him?"

"No, we were playing games. Rashid joined us, so Mo was in seventh heaven."

"Ah. I thought he had gone into the city with the other guests," Madame Al Besoud said musingly.

"Apparently not. Now he's taking Mo to see the new foal." Bridget reached for the mystery they'd been reading and opened it to where the bookmark was. "Shall I begin?"

"Would you not have preferred to go see the foal?"

"I was there when it was born. I expect I'll see it again before I leave. Don't you think it's good Mo has some private time with his father?"

"I do indeed, but wonder that you'd rather come here than spend time with them both."

"I'm dying to know how this story ends. I'll be leaving before long, so we need to make sure we finish it."

"You are kind to an old woman."

"No, it is you and Rashid who have been kind to me, inviting me here to help me deal with my papa's passing. I shall always be grateful."

By the time Bridget finished, the rain had stopped and sunshine filled the room.

"Do you think they'll still have the polo match? Or would the field be too wet?" she asked. "I've never seen one and would love to do so before I go home."

"The club has a good field, with proper drainage, since the rain has finally ended, I do believe the field will be ready by Saturday afternoon. I haven't seen a match myself in a while. They do play in the rain, but I don't like to attend those, too cold and wet. I, too, look forward to the match. And maybe expending some of that energy will help.''

''Help?'' Bridget asked.

''Tensions are running high, with Charles supposed to be squiring Elizabeth around, and making a bad job of it. Jack still hasn't asked Marie to marry him, which is what she expects. If their parents had been involved, I'm sure the matter would have been settled ages ago.''

''The famous arranged marriages,'' Bridget murmured.

Madame looked at her sharply. ''It might do some good in your country to have a few arranged marriages. The divorce rate is appalling.''

''You have no divorce in this country?''

The older woman was silent for a moment, glaring at Bridget. ''The rate does not even approach what you have.''

''My parents had a marriage that was not based on love. My father married Mum to provide a constant and steady motherly influence on Antonio's life. They had me, too. I always knew there was a lack of love from him to her. She adored him, however. Can you imagine how awful that would be?''

''There are other reasons for marriages than love,'' she stated firmly.

''Yes, but mutual love brings happiness, isn't that important, too? Were you happy in your own marriage?'' Bridget couldn't believe she'd been so rude as to ask such a personal question. Before she could apologize, however, the older woman slowly shook her head.

''No. I was infatuated with another man when I was married and could only bring my husband respect. I never developed warmer feelings for him.''

''Yet you allowed your daughter to marry without love.''

''Her father arranged her marriage.''

''And then Rashid,'' Bridget murmured, studying the book cover. ''Do you think he was happily married?''

"Not in the way his cousin, Yasmin, is. But yes, he and Fatima were happy enough."

"Yasmin?"

"The spoiled daughter of Rashid's uncle. She vowed she would only marry a man she loved. And her father allowed it."

Bridget hid a smile. Obviously Madame had been scandalized by the decision.

"And she's happy," Bridget said.

"It makes one envious to see her and her husband. They have eyes for only each other. And their new son. I expect if they were the only two people left on the face of the earth, they'd still be as happy as could be."

"That's what I want," Bridget said, trying to keep her thoughts away from Rashid. He'd made it clear love didn't figure into his plans for the future.

Bridget looked out the window at the watery sunshine. The visitors from England were leaving in a few days. She'd stay for the reception, and then make plans for returning home at the same time. The initial tearing grief of losing her papa was easing.

Being with strangers, in unfamiliar surroundings had helped. She would forever be grateful for the change, no matter what—like falling for Rashid al Halzid.

She looked quickly at Madame Al Besoud. The older woman was studying her.

"Thank you for reading that book to me, and explaining all the different ways to look at the scenes," she said. "Sometimes the meaning of the English words are not as I learned them."

She enjoyed the quiet time with Madame, as she enjoyed being with Mo. She'd miss them both when she returned home. But not as much as she would miss Rashid.

Great, she thought, the deep longing for her father would be replaced by an even deeper longing for Rashid. She had a feeling it would take longer to get over him, knowing he was living somewhere else in the world.

"Is it getting easier?" the older woman asked. "Adjusting to the loss of your father?"

"I really miss him a lot. I can't even imagine how empty my life will seem when I go home. We always had dinner together on Wednesday nights. And I often saw him and Antonio at some point over the weekend. Now, it'll be so hard for the first few weeks. When I'm here, I can almost pretend he's home in San Francisco."

Bridget wished she felt closer to her brother. Not only were the years a chasm, but he was so focused on the restaurants and business, they had only their father to tie them together. Now Papa was gone. How would she and Antonio deal together now?

"I think he was at loose ends once he turned the restaurants over to Antonio," Bridget said slowly. "I don't think retirement is for everyone. Though he did make several trips to Italy over the last few years. I know he had plenty to do with Uncle Rudolfo and Aunt Donatella, his brother and sister," Bridget explained.

Her father had liked being in the heart of things, visiting with customers, handling temperamental chefs, dealing with challenges that invigorated rather than dampened his joy for life. She missed her mother, but her father had filled that void. Now with him gone, who would fill his place?

CHAPTER EIGHT

WHEN Rashid and Mo returned to the house, it was close to dinnertime. His son had been enchanted with the new foal and had not wanted to leave.

Jack was coming down the stairs.

''So how's the new guy?'' he asked.

''Already sturdier on his feet. He's going to be a beauty,'' Rashid said. Of all his friends, Jack was the most horse mad.

''Want to go with us tomorrow?'' Rashid asked, placing his hand on Mo's shoulder.

''I'll go on my own. I'm not much into kids. Didn't you tell me he's going off to boarding school soon?''

''That's not been decided.'' Even as he said the words, he was startled to realize he didn't want Mo to go anywhere anytime soon. He was discovering his child and liking the son he'd not really known before. Seven seemed too young to be sent from home. Maybe he'd see about having him educated in Aboul Sari.

"I thought it had been decided. You certainly will be much more free without a child to worry about," Jack said.

Mo looked back and forth between the men, his face solemn.

"Mo's my son, I will always worry about him," he said resting his hand on his head. He was getting an entirely new perception about parenting. Attributable to Bridget Rossi, no doubt.

"Of course, I never meant you wouldn't. I'll see you in the salon," he said, giving a two-finger salute to Mo.

Mo and Rashid walked to the top of the stairs together and headed for Mo's bedroom. Rashid wondered if he should think about marriage. Wouldn't Mo like a mother? In the meantime, Rashid wanted to concentrate on getting to know his son.

Bridget was in a pensive mood when she returned to her room. Her visit would be coming to an end soon. She'd heard the others were planning to leave shortly after the reception. She should make her travel plans as well.

But first, she would see a polo match.

And a secret part of her yearned to experience one magical night in a party where the rest of the people were powerful, rich and beautiful. It would be several steps up from the event Richard had invited her to. She would never have the opportunity again. Could she turn her back on that?

Time enough to return to the realities of life when she did return to San Francisco. She was selfish enough to wish to see how the other half lived for one evening.

She heard a soft knock at the door. Crossing over, Bridget was delighted to find Mo standing in the hall. Glancing to his side, she spotted Rashid. He was leaning casually against the wall, watching her.

''I came to see if you wanted to have dinner with me,'' Mo said. ''Papa said I could

invite you. He said maybe you wanted someone uncompecated.''

''Compecated?'' she asked Rashid.

''Complicated. He's only five.''

''And English is his second language. I'm
still so impressed.'' She smiled at Mo. ''I
should love to have dinner with you. Will it
just be the two of us?''

Mo nodded.

''Do I need to dress?''

His eyes widened. ''Yes, you have to wear
clothes.'' He looked at his father, panic in his
eyes.

Bridget laughed. ''Then I shall wear
clothes.''

Rashid explained what she had meant and
Mo nodded solemnly. Then he smiled up at
Bridget. ''No, you don't need to dress.
Maybe you can tell me a story.''

''Mo, what did I tell you?'' Rashid asked.

''You said she was sad and I should cheer
her up. I bet she likes to tell stories, don't
you, Bridget?''

"I do. It makes me really happy to tell stories." She looked at Rashid.

"Cook made spaghetti and garlic bread, I asked her specially." Mo chattered as they walked to his suite. The table near the window had been set for two, and Rashid stopped at the doorway.

"This is just for the two of you. Will you join us later downstairs?" he asked Bridget.

"Not tonight, if it is all right with you. I shall enjoy the evening much more here than with your other guests. And I need an early night. I still plan to go to the polo match tomorrow, however."

"I want to go," Mo said. "I like polo. Are you going to play, Papa?"

"Yes. You can accompany Grandmother. Would you like to ride with her as well?" he asked Bridget.

"I would love to. She can explain the finer points of the game to me."

"As could Marie, who I believe knows as much about it as Jack does. I'll make the arrangements."

Bridget enjoyed her spaghetti dinner with Mo. She told him stories that amused him. And he told her about visiting the new foal. When Alaya came to say it was time for bed, Bridget was sorry to see the evening end.

The next morning dawned bright and sunny. Bridget was unsure what to wear to the polo match, but decided one couldn't be too dressy, traipsing around a field and sitting on the sideline watching the horses and players. She donned a gray print skirt and sleeveless yellow top. Slathering on plenty of sunscreen, she was ready.

When she entered the dining room, only Charles was present. Had the others been and gone already?

"Good morning," he said, tucking into eggs, sausages and toast.

Bridget responded and sat at the seat next to his. "I'm looking forward to seeing the game."

"It's been many years since Jack, Rashid and I played on the same team. Rashid was telling us last night that he had no difficulty in getting an opposing team. And he found another rider to make the fourth on ours. Jack is quite excited.''

''I do believe Jack would do nothing but play polo if he could,'' Bridget said.

Rashid strode into the dining room and greeted them both. Bridget's heart skipped a beat. He wore classic riding britches and high, polished black boots. His red polo shirt, aptly named, she thought, covered his muscular chest and arms. He looked good enough to eat. She had never seen him look so sexy or approachable. She forgot he was a sheikh of an important country whose oil reserves kept him in more money than she'd ever see. She forgot about his ideas on love and marriage, or his beautiful first wife.

All she could do was stare and hope she didn't give away the myriad of feelings that overwhelmed her.

She loved him.

She wanted him for herself, forever.

And she knew he was never going to be hers.

Rashid looked at her when he sat. "Are you feeling all right?"

She looked away, smiling brightly. "Definitely. And I'm looking forward to the polo match," Bridget said, feeling her face flame. Thank goodness he couldn't read minds. What was she going to do? She couldn't be in love with a sheikh.

Jack entered, wearing attire identical to Rashid's. While he looked fit and trim, he couldn't hold a candle to Rashid in sheer animal magnetism.

In only a few moments the dining room was crowded with guests, all chatting furiously about the upcoming match. Charles obviously enjoyed the game almost as much as Jack and was holding forth on blunders made in the past, some of which he himself had done. It was in good fun, and laughter frequent.

As soon as Bridget finished eating, she rose, hoping to leave unnoticed. But Rashid spoke before she could reach the door.

"Bridget, my grandmother will be ready to leave at nine."

She turned and nodded.

"Bring Mo down to see the horses if you would once we are all on the field. He'll like that," he said.

"Are you sure a polo match is suitable for a young child?" Marie asked. "He will probably be bored and then fretful."

"I think he'll enjoy it. Would you like to come down to see the horses as well?" Rashid asked.

"We'll see." She grinned at Jack. "Maybe I will come to kiss my man for luck."

Bridget slipped through the door and headed for the stairs. She felt a momentary pang for Rashid. Fatima had not cared for his horses. Marie obviously supported Jack and his interests. Would he find a woman one day who would share his interests? Who would love him as much as she did?

The limousine that carried Madame Al Besoud was luxurious. Bridget knew she'd always love this mode of travel and tried to imagine having a limousine and driver at her disposal in San Francisco. Sure would solve parking problems.

Mo was excited, bouncing in his seat, looking out the window, and chatting a mile a minute, sometimes in Arabic, sometimes in English.

"Do you think Papa will let me ride on his horse with him?" he asked as they turned into the grounds of the polo club.

"If he and his friends win, maybe you can ride the victory lap," Bridget said. "We can ask him."

"Victory lap?" Madame asked.

Bridget looked at them both. "It's a rodeo custom, I guess. When a cowboy wins an event, he then takes a ride around the arena, usually waving his hat to all the applause. Maybe they don't do that in polo."

"You know cowboys?" Mo asked, fascinated.

"Not really. I live in the city. But there is a terrific rodeo each year at the Cow Palace near San Francisco, and I usually go. I always wanted a horse when I was little.''

''Now do you have one?'' he asked.

''No. There's no place for me to keep one where I live. So I go and watch the rodeo and wander around the exhibits.''

''I can ride. I have my own pony,'' Mo said.

''I know, I saw him when I was in the stable.''

''He's bigger than the new baby horse, but the baby will grow up bigger.''

''I know, but your pony is still a wonderful animal.''

The car had stopped and the driver opened the rear door, assisting Madame Al Besoud from the limo. He then offered assistance to Bridget, while Mo scrambled out himself.

Stands were built on both sides of a wide expanse of grassy field. At either end, goal posts delineating the scoring area rose to a height of eight feet. Bridget gazed around in wonder. There were already quite a number of people on both sides of the field, not filling the stands, but certainly making good use of them.

"I didn't expect so many people," she murmured as Madame led the way to the box seats near the center of the stands.

"There are many people who enjoy watching games. Though this is not a regularly scheduled one on the club's calendar, I'm sure everyone heard Rashid and his English friends wanted a match." She nodded to acquaintances as she climbed the short set of stairs leading to a box with comfortable stadium seats. Elizabeth and Marie were already there, avidly watching the players warm up on the playing field.

Bridget walked beside Madame Al Besoud, sitting next to her when she chose a seat in the front row. Mo hung over the railing, waving at his father.

A moment later, Rashid rode his powerful black horse to the edge of the field and gestured for Mo and Bridget to join him.

He dismounted when they drew near, and Bridget was struck by his ease around the horses. For a moment the polo attire faded and she could see him as he might have been a hundred years ago—a warrior riding the deserts to defend his people. Instead of the helmet and red jersey, she envisioned him in flowing robes, riding his black steed across the burning sand. Her heart cartwheeled and began a rapid beat. She wished she could see him striding into some tent, claiming all he saw for himself. She'd love to be one of the spoils of war for this man.

"Papa, Bridget said you can take me on your victory lap," Mo exclaimed running up to his father.

"Victory lap?"

When Bridget explained, he nodded. "You have a lot of faith we will win, promising such a thing."

"I didn't promise, but I do think you'll win. I suspect you win most of your matches."

Jack rode up and dismounted. "Come to wish us luck?" he asked, grinning at Bridget and Mo.

"Of course, but I bet luck has little to do with it. You'll win easily, right?"

"I hope it won't be too easy, I like a challenge. But I do like to win."

Marie waved from the stands and rose. Bridget watched as she spoke with Elizabeth, who then joined her. In only minutes, they joined them at the edge of the field.

"I wanted to give you a good luck kiss," Marie said as she reached Jack. She encircled his neck with her arms and pulled his head down for a kiss. Her hat sheltered them a little from the view of the rest of the world.

Bridget took Mo's hand. "We better return to our seat."

"Why is that lady kissing him?" he asked, refusing to move, fascinated by Marie and Jack's embrace.

"For luck, darling boy," Marie said when she broke the kiss. "He and your father will win the match."

"Then Bridget should kiss Papa for luck."

Bridget looked at Rashid, and met his amused eyes.

"No, Mo. Too much is not good. Your father doesn't need any kisses. Come, let's return to our seats." With that she turned and headed for the stands.

Rashid caught her arm and stopped her. "A team can never have too many kisses for luck, you know."

She looked at his mouth then met his eyes. "I'm not kissing you."

"Then I'll kiss you," he said, and did. His mouth covered hers in an explosive kiss that she felt to her toes. Almost before she could move, he released her and laughed.

"My luck is running high now," he said to Mo.

The match was thrilling. Madame explained the different plays, the scoring, and penalties. But it was the thundering sound of horses' hooves, the thwack of a mallet against the ball, and the cheers of the crowds which kept the game exciting. By the end, she could almost understand some of the plays.

Her eyes never left Rashid. He made it look like child's play, scoring two of the five goals his team made. The opposition scored only three.

When it was over, Rashid motioned for Mo to join him, and he rode his horse around the field in a victory lap.

Madame Al Besoud watched with a small smile.

"You've given them both a memory they will treasure," she said softly to Bridget. "And maybe started a new tradition with the club."

"Me?"

"Rashid didn't see Mo much before you came. I believe he will now spend more time with him. He is an enchanting child, as you know. I'm happy his father now recognizes that. Fatima kept the baby with her, selfishly, I believe. I think Rashid thought child care was only for women."

"And you think men should be involved?"

"Don't you?"

"Of course, but I'm an American, we always are looking to have the fathers involved. I wasn't sure other cultures would see it the same way," Bridget said.

"Yet every parent wants the best for his or her child. You've shown Rashid he can enjoy his son before he is an adult. Come, my car awaits."

"What about Mo?"

"His father can see to him. You are not his nursemaid."

CHAPTER NINE

MEMBERS of the opposing polo team and their wives had been invited to dinner. Afterward the entire match was rehashed in the drawing room. Jack was in high spirits after the game, and Marie matched his exuberance. Charles and Elizabeth were a bit more subdued, but everyone in the losing team took the ribbing in good humor.

Bridget enjoyed the evening, though she had little to contribute. It was interesting to see Rashid with members of his own social circle, not just his friends from England.

Tomorrow evening was the state reception, and the day after that Rashid had invited them all to the beach. By Wednesday of next week, the other guests would be leaving. Bridget planned to ride to the airport with them. She needed to book a flight home first thing Monday morning before they left for the beach. She hoped she could get a seat on such short notice.

For a moment the thought of returning to San Francisco saddened her. She still had the task ahead of her of clearing her father's things, donating the clothes that still had life in them, and tossing those with no further value.

She knew Antonio wouldn't want to help, he'd view that as women's work. It would be easier if they did it together, remembering their father's life, sharing special incidences with each other. Maybe she could talk him into helping her.

Sunday evening Bridget was ready to leave before the appointed time. She stood in front of the floor-length mirror in her room gazing at the sight that met her eyes. Marie had insisted on doing her hair. It swept up, with large curls clustered at the top and a few tendrils that curved down around her face, just brushing her shoulders when she turned her head.

The cream-colored dress was a dream, as lovely as the first moment she'd seen it. It brought out the delicate color on her cheeks, blush not needed. She loved the way it fit, the way it felt like a cloud against her skin, and revealed every feminine curve.

She left her room to go down the hall to see Mo, having promised she would tell him good-night before she left. When she knocked on his door, Rashid opened it. He was dressed in formal attire, and looked stunning. She'd once wished he'd dress informally all the time so she could enjoy the view. Now she knew these clothes made the man. He was devastating. She felt her heart rate increase as a wave of sadness swept through her. She was going home soon, probably never to see him again. How would she stand it?

Rashid stared at the vision before him. Bridget looked as beautiful as any woman he'd ever seen. The dress had been made for her. It could never give that glow of beauty to anyone else so well. Her hair was done up, making his fingers itch to let it down until it tumbled over her creamy shoulders. He knew its softness, he wanted to feel it again.

''I came to bid Mo good night,'' she said softly. Her eyes seemed larger than normal, color flushed her cheeks.

All thoughts of duty and obligations momentarily fled. He wanted to take her some place private and spend the evening alone, with just her. For a moment he said nothing, then at her quizzical look, he spoke.

''I, too, came to say good night.'' The urge to shut the door, order Mo to his bedroom and kiss her all night long was almost too strong to resist. But he had duties and responsibilities to see to. He didn't have the luxury of doing only what he wanted.

''Bridget, you look beautiful,'' Mo said, coming up to stand by his father. ''Like a fairy princess.''

She smiled, and Rashid felt a reaction deep within. She smiled often at his son. The prick of jealousy he felt was irrational. But it was there. He wanted her to smile at him that way.

"I don't know about that, but it is a lovely dress, isn't it? My cousin bought it for me. I love it."

Bridget twirled around, showing off the dress for Mo. Rashid was sorry for the loss of her father, but suddenly he considered the unexpected bonus of Bridget's presence in his home. He never would have met her had her cousin not asked him to take her to the funeral.

"How nice of Francesca, and did she get you the other things from the boutique?" he asked for clarity.

"Yes. I offered to pay, but she said she wouldn't hear of it. I never would have bought so much on my own."

"Mo, tell Bridget good night, but no hugs, you don't want to risk getting anything sticky on her beautiful gown."

"Nonsense, a hug is worth more than a dress any day," Bridget said, opening her arms to his son.

Mo's impish grin let Rashid know he delighted in her contradicting his father. Bridget seemed to have that knack.

"I have butterflies in my stomach," she said a few moments later as they walked along the hall toward the stairs.

"Because?"

"Because of the reception, of course. What if I make a total idiot of myself? Or spill a drink on an ambassador. That could cause an international incident. Or what if I become tongue-tied or am the only American someone meets. They'll think we're all dumber than dirt," she said.

He wanted to laugh at her assessment, but knew she was serious. She didn't seem to know how easily she could charm anyone with her forthright talk, her honesty, and her delight in everything she saw.

"First of all, if you spill something, we'll have it mopped up. Ambassadors are human just as we are. I am sure somewhere in their lives, they've even spilled a drink or two."

"I don't think you get appointed an ambassador if you're in the habit of spilling drinks," she said.

He did laugh at that. "Not in the habit, but it happens. Secondly, most people attending tonight have met other Americans. You will be a shining representative of your country."

She stopped and looked at him, her delight clearly visible in her expression. "Why, Rashid, that's a lovely thing to say. Thank you."

He took a step forward, unable to resist. One kiss, that's all he'd take. It would have to last the night, but certainly he was entitled to one kiss.

Marie came from her room at that moment, spotting the two of them and calling a greeting. Rashid took a deep breath. That kiss would have to wait. He nodded to Marie.

"You look beautiful," he said sincerely.

"Thank you, Rashid, but I do believe your American guest will be the belle of the ball. The dress is fabulous," she said appraising Bridget.

"I love it. Thank you again for helping with my hair. I feel up to anything, I think," Bridget responded.

"Are we all traveling together?" Marie asked, as they started down the stairs.

"I will be traveling with my grandmother. We need to arrive before the invited guests. I have arranged for two more cars for the rest of you," Rashid said.

Charles and Elizabeth were in the salon standing near one of the windows, deep in discussion. Jack had not yet come down. Rashid hoped his grandmother would join them soon, it was time for them to leave.

"I'm quite looking forward to meeting your parents again," Marie said. "I met them when they came to Paris a couple of years ago," she explained to Bridget.

"Indeed. I'm sure they'll be happy to see all my guests, and meet Bridget," Rashid said.

"Will your cousin Yasmin and her husband be there?" Bridget asked.

"Yes, I'll make sure you meet her. You two will have a lot in common, I think."

Rashid checked his watch just as his grandmother entered the room. She looked elegant as always, dressed in black with the jewels she favored at her throat and wrist.

"I did not keep you waiting, I trust," she said.

"Not at all. The car is out front. Are you ready to leave?"

"Yes." She smiled at Bridget. "I shall be happy to introduce you to my daughter and maybe you can find Yasmin and you two will find a meeting of the minds."

"I told her the same thing," Rashid said.

"I shall look forward to it," Bridget replied, smiling at the older woman.

"Until later," he said.

Bridget watched the two leave, trying to still the butterflies in her stomach. She couldn't help thinking about the fiasco with Richard. She'd be careful to take nothing that could spill or drop, and she'd be fine. She hoped.

Thanks to dinner the previous evening, she now knew a few more people who would be attending.

She hoped she could make it through the evening without totally disgracing her host.

''I love events like this,'' Marie said as they pulled silently away from the villa.

''I don't.'' Bridget would have been just as happy staying in and reading a good book.

''Why ever not? Lots of interesting people to talk to.''

''Interesting men to meet,'' Elizabeth murmured with a sidelong glance at Charles.

''I'm not big on chitchat with strangers, unless it has to do with books or other things with the library.'' She was not going to tell these sophisticated people of her gaffe at Richard's party. It was bad enough to remember it in vivid detail.

''Did you see the diamonds Madame Al Besoud was wearing?'' Elizabeth asked. ''I expect all the women in their family have scads of jewels, diamonds, emeralds and rubies. Do you think they have these receptions just so they can wear all that loot?''

Marie laughed softly. ''Wouldn't be surprised. Why don't you buy me something nice like Madame's necklace,'' she asked Jack.

He groaned. ''If I wanted to spend a king's ransom I could. But then I couldn't afford to eat for a year.''

''Ah, poor baby.''

''Not so poor, just not in Rashid's league.''

''Few are,'' Charles commented.

Another reminder of the gulf between them, Bridget reminded herself. Any feelings she was having toward Rashid needed to be nipped in the bud. He had kindly offered her a place to visit while the immediate shock of her papa's death faded. It was a kindness she wouldn't forget. But there was nothing more to it.

Their arrival at their destination saved Bridget further depressing thoughts. There was nothing wrong with her life in San Francisco. The sooner she returned home, the better.

The palace was ablaze with light. Cars and limousines were lined up on the driveway, discharging their passengers and then smoothly moving on. Several couples stood near the entry talking. Others were entering through the ornate double doors held wide by men in uniform.

Bridget took it all in, imprinting it to memory to tell her friends when she returned home. They would demand to hear every detail. And she wanted to forget nothing. For once she could imagine how Cinderella must have felt showing up for the ball.

Head held high, her resolve firmly in place, she followed the others into the State Hall. There was a receiving line comprised of His Excellency, Sheikh Mohammedan Al Halzid, his three sons and the visiting ambassador. Rashid was a familiar face, but the others were unknown. Bridget could see the family resemblance, and noted all the sons favored their father.

Once beyond the receiving line, she took in the splendor of the room, with crystal chandeliers suspended from the high ceiling, ornate gold leaf decorating the trim and the silk-covered walls, shimmering in the light.

Charles and Elizabeth joined her. ''I say, this is fabulous,'' he said, gazing around. ''I've visited Rashid several times over the years, but never been here before.''

Elizabeth looked animated for the first time Bridget remembered. It was not crowded, yet there were many people in the large room. Dresses of all styles and fabrics were worn with aplomb. Jewels sparkled. Voices spoke a myriad of languages. Bridget had never attended an event like it.

''Miss, your presence is requested,'' a man in military uniform stepped beside Bridget.

''Me?'' she asked.

''I will escort you.'' He offered his arm. She took it and they crossed through the crowd. He led her to Madame Al Besoud.

She was talking with another two women, one about Bridget's age, one older.

"Delivered as requested," he said in English when they reached the threesome. He gave a slight bow.

"Thank you." Madame Al Besoud reached out to draw Bridget into the group. "My daughter, Sadi, and Rashid's cousin, Yasmin. This is the American woman I was telling you about, Bridget Rossi."

"How do you do?" Bridget greeted her hostess and the young woman beaming a bright smile her way.

"I have visited San Francisco," Sadi al Halzid said. "It is a lovely city, though I didn't like the cold fog."

Bridget laughed. "It can be cool, but we call it nature's air-conditioning. It does keep the temperatures down. Rashid has graciously given me a short tour of Aboul Sari. I like the oases, but not the desert so much."

"Me, either. Give me air-conditioning," Yasmin said. "Did he take you to the bazaar?"

Bridget shook her head.

"Then let me tell you the best times to go and where to look for the most fabulous materials and rugs. Better yet, shall we arrange a time to visit together? I'll show you the best stalls." Soon Yasmin and Bridget found chairs and sat for conversation. Time flew by. Time and time again waiters would stop offering beverages or hors d'oeuvres. Bridget declined each offering.

At last Yasmin questioned her refusal. "I'm starving, but don't want to take anything if you don't," she said. "Are you on some diet or something?"

"No, I'm afraid I'll spill everything." Despite her reluctance to tell about the last formal reception she attended, she found it easy to relate the event to Yasmin, embellishing it until both of them were laughing by the time she finished. Had she put the trauma behind her at last?

"The next dance is mine," Rashid said appearing suddenly in front of them.

Bridget looked up, surprised to see him. She looked around, not seeing anyone dancing.

"I didn't know there was dancing."

"In the ballroom, adjacent to this room." He greeted his cousin. "Where is Mikeil? I'm surprised to find you two separated."

"It was a hardship, but I've survived. Your father had some shipping people he wanted Mikeil to speak to. He will find me when he's done."

"Undoubtedly. In the meantime, may I take Bridget?"

"That's her decision, but I can't see why she would want to go off with you when she and I were having such a great talk," Yasmin said cheekily.

Rashid offered his hand and Bridget put hers into his. She rose and smiled at Yasmin. "I've enjoyed visiting, do call if we can go shopping on Tuesday. Otherwise, another time." She knew there would be no other time.

Yasmin rose as well, leaning to kiss Rashid on the cheek. ''I like your guest. You should have more visiting like her. You two have fun. I'll make sure you meet Mikeil before the night is over.''

Rashid tucked her hand into the crook of his elbow as they crossed the reception area. The noise level was louder than earlier. She glanced around, surprised to realize how crowded the room had become.

The next room held almost an equal number of people dancing to the music played at one end of the large ballroom. Rashid swept her into his arms and moved them onto the dance floor moving in perfect time to the slow tempo.

Bridget was in heaven. She rested her forehead against his chin, breathed in his scent. His legs brushed against hers as they swayed in time to the melody. Her hand held in his tightened slightly when he brought her against him with his other arm. They moved as one.

"I take it you have finished your duties in the reception line," she said a moment later.

"Yes, the formal line disbursed. My father is now introducing the ambassador to close friends, and people who need personal contact. The discussions will last most of the evening, but I'm not needed for that."

"I met your mother, and of course Yasmin. I liked them both. I hope I see them again before I leave."

"Yasmin will surely call. She has a wide circle of friends you might like. And she loves to shop."

"So I gathered." Bridget loved the implicit intimacy of talking softly while they danced. His breath caressed her cheek when he spoke. She felt as if they were in a world of their own.

When the song ended, Rashid introduced her to friends nearby. Bridget danced every dance, sometimes with men who spoke English, other times with men who did not. She enjoyed herself and the specter of

Richard and their last night together faded completely.

Rashid claimed her for another dance near midnight. The lights had been dimmed, and the music was unfamiliar to her, but she didn't hesitate a moment. Not a single partner all evening had compared to him.

"My grandmother left for home an hour ago. You must let me know when you wish to return," he said.

"How long will the reception last?" she asked.

"The ambassador has already left. My parents will leave soon, as some attending will not depart until after they have gone. The rest will stay as long as they are enjoying themselves."

"I'm having a wonderful time, but I will probably want to leave soon. My feet are killing me," she confessed ruefully. She had never danced so much in one night, and the lovely shoes weren't designed for hours on her feet.

He stopped. "Shall we leave now?"

''No! I want to finish our dance.'' In fact, if she was dancing with Rashid, she'd go on all night, hurt feet or not.

He held her closely, tucking their hands in near to their shoulders, his left arm holding her. Bridget thought he kissed her hair, but wasn't sure. She pulled back to look at him, their faces so close she would only have to lean forward an inch or two to kiss him herself.

If protocol didn't dictate discretion, she might have availed herself of the opportunity. But he was the son of the ruling sheikh. They were in too public a place to risk embarrassing him. But she couldn't help wishing he would kiss her. That would make it all right.

As if he read her mind, he closed the gap and covered her mouth with his. Bridget gave a soft sigh of delight and kissed him back. For the moment she refused to think about the other people in the ballroom or the consequences of such a reckless public display.

She savored every second, relished every touching point between them. Tonight was magical, tomorrow would be time enough to return to reality.

"Rashid, can you have a car brought round for me? I'm leaving. I've had enough of Charles humiliating me in front of every-one!" Elizabeth said, popping the fantasy bubble Bridget floated in.

CHAPTER TEN

RASHID released Bridget and turned to Elizabeth. Assessing her anger, he quickly escorted her from the center of the ballroom, Bridget beside him.

"I'm happy to take you home now, if you like. I'll see to the car immediately. What happened?"

Elizabeth was almost in tears, but anger kept her in control. "I am supposed to be Charles's date to this event. Heck, to the house party. I thought this would be the romantic place he'd propose to me. Instead, he took one look at Francesca Bianchetti and had eyes only for her while she was here. Tonight he's flirting with every pretty woman in the place, and virtually ignoring me. I've had enough. I wish to return to the villa and pack to leave. I'm not going to stay another moment!"

"Come, we will leave. Bridget?"

"Yes, I'm ready to go, too," she said, feeling guilty over her cousin's part in Elizabeth's problems. But everybody at the villa had known Francesca was only flirting. Surely it was harmless. Francesca was too wrapped up in her career to become involved with anyone.

In no time Rashid had summoned a car and they were on their way back to the villa. Elizabeth said nothing after they started, but Bridget knew her anger simmered by the way she clenched her fists in her lap.

"If you feel you wish to leave in the morning, I will take you to the airport," Rashid said at last.

"I wish to leave tonight." Anger laced her voice.

"It's after midnight," Bridget said. Did Elizabeth not realize how late it was?

"I don't care. I don't wish to stay another night. Charles has no feelings for me. I'd just as soon leave before he returns. It's too bad your troublesome cousin isn't still here to console him," Elizabeth said.

"What?" Bridget couldn't believe she'd heard right.

"That's enough," Rashid said calmly.

"Either you are as blind as Charles, or you don't care, Rashid. Are you so besotted by a beautiful face that rational thought goes out the window? Francesca uses people. You, Charles. Who knows where she is now. She lets you buy her expensive clothes and take her to exotic places and gives you what in return? She dumps her cousin on you, letting you buy her clothes, entertain her. What next, an Italian grandmother, an aging aunt?"

"What clothes?" Bridget felt a sinking in her heart. "Elizabeth, what are you talking about?"

"The very ones you're wearing, of course. Don't tell me you didn't know Rashid paid the bill," she scoffed, clearly on a roll.

"Francesca bought them."

"Tell her," Elizabeth said, glaring at Rashid. "Tell her how Francesca delights in spending your money as if it were her own. Or is she just anticipating a happy event the rest of us don't know about?''

Bridget turned to him in horror. ''Rashid, you didn't pay for these clothes, did you?''

''It was nothing, Bridget. I was happy to do it,'' he said.

''I thought Francesca bought them. I can't have you buying me clothes.'' Bridget couldn't believe what she was hearing. She was certain Francesca had purchased the clothes. How could she let Rashid pay for them? He hadn't even known her but a day when she'd bought them. It wasn't some casual meaningless gesture to the cousin of a friend. They had cost a lot of money!

''It doesn't matter,'' he said, his voice tightening in irritation.

''It certainly matters to me. I'll pay you back,'' she said, embarrassed.

Elizabeth gave a harsh laugh. ''That's easier said than done, my dear. That's a haute couture gown you're wearing...it probably cost more than a librarian makes in a year.

And how about that silk blouse you wore the other day, it probably—''

''Enough!'' Rashid said. ''Elizabeth, you will kindly mind your own business. Bridget, I do not wish to hear about repaying me for the clothes. Is that clear to both of you?''

Bridget nodded, fuming. She tried to remember exactly why she'd thought Francesca footed the bill. When she'd asked, her cousin had said it was all taken care of. Naturally Bridget assumed she'd meant her cousin was taking care of the bill. She never would have accepted the dresses had she known Rashid was paying. Francesca had put her in an untenable position. Maybe she was used to taking gifts like this from men, but Bridget certainly wasn't.

''I still wish to leave tonight,'' Elizabeth said stiffly.

''There are no planes for England at this time,'' Rashid said reasonably.

''Then I'll find a hotel near the airport.''

Bridget gazed out the window. For a moment, she wished she could join Elizabeth in leaving. She was totally embarrassed. Did everyone at the villa know she'd bought the clothes on Rashid's money? Was she the only one who hadn't known?

They arrived at the villa in silence. Rashid helped Bridget from the car, turning then to assist Elizabeth. He sent the driver back for the rest of the guests and escorted them inside the house.

Elizabeth went straight for the stairs. ''I'm packing.''

''Elizabeth, I will have a car for you at eight in the morning. I cannot let you leave now,'' Rashid said.

She hesitated a moment on the bottom step, then nodded. ''Very well, first thing in the morning, then.'' She ran up the stairs and disappeared around the corner.

Rashid looked at Bridget. ''Are you dashing off to bed now, or would you stay with me a while? Would you care for a drink or something to eat?''

She shook her head. While eating sparingly at the reception, lest she spill something, she was too keyed up to be hungry.

"I'm not quite ready to go up," she said. Nor ready to drop the matter of the clothes, no matter what Rashid said. She would come up with a way to repay him!

"About the dresses—" she started.

He placed a finger across her lips. "I do not wish to discuss the dresses. Enjoy them. You look lovely in them and despite what Elizabeth said, they did not cost a fortune. Come, join me for a little while. We will have the salon to ourselves, I'm sure. Grandmother would have retired upon her return and the others won't arrive for a while."

She didn't want to drop the subject, but temporarily gave in. As they walked into the salon, her curiosity peaked. "What do you suppose happened between Charles and Elizabeth?" Bridget asked as they entered the dimly lit room. The French doors were opened to the night breeze, the path to the gardens visible.

"I expect he paid more attention to other women than Elizabeth wanted. I know she came expecting a marriage proposal, and he has not delivered.''

''Cynical Rashid, a proposal should be romantic and wonderful, not something delivered,'' Bridget said, trying to concentrate on the conversation at hand and not dwell on the other matter.

''Should he have swept her off her feet, strewn roses along her path and wined and dined her in style before losing his freedom forever?'' he asked whimsically.

She laughed. ''I can't imagine Charles being that romantic. And I question your use of the term loss of freedom. Didn't you enjoy freedom when you were married?''

''Yes, but look at Mikeil, he can't take a step without Yasmin.''

''I think it's very romantic. They adore each other and don't mind who knows it.'' Wistfully she gazed off to the garden. ''That's the kind of love I hoped to have one day,'' she said softly.

''Hoped as in past tense?'' Rashid questioned.

She shook off her yearning and corrected herself. "Hope for. I think I'd rather remain alone than marry where there was no love." Or where the love was all on one side as her mother had known.

"Come, let's walk in the garden. The warm weather won't last forever." He tucked her hand in the crook of his arm and led her into the night. Night blooming jasmine sweetened the air. The wind rustled the leaves gently, providing a magical melody. Bridget found another moment she wished to capture for all eternity.

"Did you enjoy the reception?" he asked as they turned a corner away from the house. Without the illumination from the salon, the night became darker, despite the pathway lights.

"I did, unexpectedly. Thank you for inviting me. I will have lots of things to tell my friends when I return home. Once again I must thank you for your invitation to visit. It has helped me get beyond the immediate pain of Papa's death."

Of course, now she'd have the pain of heartbreak to deal with, but that was something he must never know. She craved his company so much. Surely a walk in the gardens couldn't hurt anything. One night wouldn't matter in the greater scheme of things. And it would add another memory to treasure.

He stopped and turned to look at her, cupping her face in his hands. "It is my pleasure to have you here, Bridget. Remember that." Then he kissed her.

It was unexpected, and most welcomed. Bridget kissed him back, delighting in the embrace when he wrapped his arms around her and held her close. Moments later she felt his fingers in her hair, the pins flung away, the tresses tumbling to her shoulders.

He pulled back and looked at her in the faint light, quiet satisfaction in his eyes. "I've wanted to do that since I first saw you tonight." He threaded his fingers through the soft strands, sending sensuous shivers of delight down her spine.

"I wish I could see it spread on my pillow, see it in the moonlight, in the early dawn. Stay with me, Bridget, after the others leave on Wednesday. Stay a little longer."

She pulled free, staring at him. For a moment hope blossomed. Then what he said penetrated. As well as what he hadn't said. Was he suggesting an affair? She was dismayed. Had her letting him kiss her given him the impression she would condone such a relationship once it was made?

"No, I can't stay. I need to go home." Bridget backed away another step, yearning for him to sweep aside any doubts she had, tell her he loved her beyond measure and wanted her to marry him and have a half dozen children with him.

"Nothing pressing awaits you at your home. Stay just a little while longer," he urged.

So much for dreams. A little while longer was nowhere near a proposal. Not even close to declaring love.

"I think we had…" she began.

He raised his head, listening. Once again Bridget saw him as a warrior, scenting danger, poised to take action. She wished for a moment things were simpler, that she didn't care so much. Didn't wish so strongly she dare take him up on his offer and say to hell with the consequences.

But she couldn't. How much deeper in love would she fall if she stayed? And the outcome was already assured. He didn't love her. She wouldn't give her all like her mother had, only to be met with indifferent affection. It was too hard.

''The others have returned,'' he said.

Her hands covered her hair, pulling it back. ''I can't go in looking like this,'' she protested.

He frowned, then turned back toward the house. ''Very well, wait here. Once I get them all upstairs, you can come in with no one the wiser.''

Bridget followed at a distance, stopping when she could see into the lighted salon. Charles and Jack were arguing, Marie was yawning widely. When Rashid stepped in from the terrace, Bridget instinctively stepped back, even though she knew no one could see her in the darkness.

She couldn't hear the conversation, but it was only moments later when they all left the salon.

Had she made the right choice? She licked her lips, still tasting him, the yearning in her heart growing. She'd never been with a man who touched her so deeply, but it was like a fairy tale. Surely once she was back home, all this would fade and she'd forget the feelings that threatened to overwhelm her tonight.

Waiting a few minutes longer, Bridget brushed back her hair the best she was able and entered the salon. Was someone coming to lock the doors? She pulled them shut behind her.

When she reached the entryway, she paused, listening. The house was silent.

She climbed the stairs quietly, feeling as if she were sneaking in from an illicit date or something. The charm of the evening had faded. She was tired, drained, and longed for bed.

The next morning, Bridget rose early. She had not slept well. A day at the beach was just what she needed. Rashid had said Mo might be included. She'd spend the day with the child, and ruthlessly ignore Rashid.

Tomorrow she'd do her final packing and depart on Wednesday. She did not yet have a reservation. That she must remedy immediately. Leaving her room, she started downstairs when Elizabeth left her room farther along the hallway. She was dressed for travel.

"Elizabeth, how did you get a reservation?" Bridget asked when she drew near.

"Phone." She walked with her head held high, but Bridget could see the swollen eyes from crying.

"The operators speak English?" Bridget hurried to keep up with her.

"Ask for an English speaking attendant when you dial, they'll connect you. You'll have to use the phone in Rashid's study.'' Elizabeth paused at the top of the stairs and turned to Bridget. ''I apologize for last night. I saw after I spoke that you really didn't know your cousin was allowing Rashid to foot the bill for all the clothes. You did nothing wrong and I apologize for lumping you in with your cousin.''

''I'm sorry for the trouble she caused,'' Bridget offered gently.

Elizabeth's eyes filled with tears. ''Me, too,'' she said, and turned to descend.

Bridget watched her leave. She hadn't a clue where Rashid's study was. Sighing softly, she knew she would have to wait to ask him when she saw him.

It was early, but Mo would likely be awake. Maybe she could eat breakfast with him and avoid the discussion that was sure to take place in the dining room when the others learned of Elizabeth's departure. She could imagine the speculation that would result. Would Charles even notice?

Mo was delighted to see her and it did Bridget's heart good to have at least one member of the family open about his feelings.

She chatted with Mo while they ate breakfast, all the while wishing Rashid had joined them.

Wasn't she setting herself up for the same kind of heartache her mother had endured? There was no question her mother had loved Antonio as much as she had loved Bridget. And she had tried so hard to please Papa, hoping he would love her as much as he had loved his beautiful Isabella.

Bridget knew better than to fall in the same trap, but despite all her intentions, there were a lot of similarities. Of course, the primary one was missing—where Rashid asked her to marry him.

He was attracted to her, he made no effort to hide that. But physical attraction was fleeting. She wanted a love so powerful it would endure forever. Was that too much to ask? Only with Rashid. He had loved his first wife.

And nothing indicated he was looking for an-other one.

Any ideas along those lines were purely wishful thinking. Instead she should be mak-ing plans to return home. She had her life to live.

"Do you go to the sea a lot?" Mo asked. "Alaya showed me where you live, right on the water."

"San Francisco is on the tip of a peninsula, so we have lots of water around us. But I don't go to the beach often. The water is very cold, not warm like the Med."

"Sometimes my bath gets cold."

"And then you're glad to get out, right?"

He nodded.

"So you see why I don't go to the ocean often. Do you like the beach?"

"I do. I make castles, and dig for water and dive through the waves like Papa said he would do if the big wave came."

"You are a good swimmer. But don't go far from shore."

"Oh, no, or I might be taken for a long ride and it would be hard for Papa to find me."

Bridget smiled at his solemn tone. Obviously someone had taught him well.

When everyone was ready to leave, they gathered in the foyer. Rashid snapped orders as to who would ride with whom. He and Bridget would take his sports car, he informed the group. Marie smiled. Jack offered to drive it back to save Rashid the chore. Charles looked uncomfortable.

Bridget wondered if she should not have skipped breakfast. Maybe Marie would tell her later what had transpired.

The drive was exhilarating. She wondered if she should consider getting a convertible when she returned home. It felt so free with the wind in her hair, the sun warming her shoulders and the terrific view she had of everything.

Of course it might not be the same having a car of her own with no special person to share it with.

"You look sad, what is the matter?" Rashid asked, flicking her a glance.

"Just feeling sad this special time is almost over. I need to make sure I can get reservations for Wednesday. I have an open ended ticket."

"I wish you would stay."

"I have enjoyed myself," she said politely. "I will miss all this when I'm gone." *And you!*

"Then, don't go. Stay, Bridget. Stay with me."

"For how long?" *Please say forever. Tell me you love me,* she willed.

"As long as we both wish it. At least through the summer. I can show you more of Aboul Sari, take you on my yacht. When the others leave, my grandmother will also be returning to her home. It would just be you and me."

"And Mo," she said. "Thank you for the offer, but I need to get home."

"Don't say no without thinking about it," he almost ordered.

"Very well, I'll think about it before I say no." She tried to keep it light, lest he guess how much she longed to do just what he asked. But no words of love had passed his lips, and she knew she wasn't cut out for a one-sided relationship.

CHAPTER ELEVEN

WHEN they arrived at the beach, there were already several cars parked in a paved area off the road. Before them lay a stretch of pristine white sand beach, and beyond the gorgeous blue of the Mediterranean Sea. Except for several chairs already set up near the water, and the open tent shading tables of food, the place was deserted.

''This is beautiful,'' she said when he stopped the car near the sand. ''Doesn't anyone else think so?''

''I hope all my guests do.''

''It's your private beach?'' she asked, looking at him.

''My family's, yes.''

Oh wow, as far as she could see in either direction was only empty sand and cloudless sky. Imagine having a perfect beach for only one family. It was mind-boggling.

261

She grabbed her tote bag and joined Rashid. The sand was warm underfoot. They walked to the tent, where several tables and chairs were arranged. Piles of fluffy towels were stacked near the edge. Food was being unwrapped on the long buffet table.

The chaise longues were nearer the water's edge.

''How perfect,'' she said, taking in everything. She'd never imagined such a magnificent spread in the middle of the beach. Usually she and her friends either roasted hot dogs, or brought sandwiches when they went to the beach. And the only time the beaches near San Francisco were totally empty was when the weather was terrible.

Before long the others joined them. Mo was excited about swimming and despite Rashid's comment that Bridget needn't take him, because Alaya was there to watch his son, she took the little boy's hand and headed for the water. In only moments, Rashid joined them.

It was like heaven. The sun warm overhead and the water a silky sensation against her skin. The temperature enough to cool her off without being too cold to stay in a long time.

The three of them played for a while, until Mo tired. Rashid sent him back to Alaya, and swam next to Bridget.

"It's so buoyant," she commented, lying back to float on the top of the water. It was almost as flat as glass.

"Much nicer than the stretch of Pacific Ocean by San Francisco," she murmured.

"Another enticement to stay," he said.

She dropped her feet and came upright in the water. Rashid was closer than she expected.

"There's much more enticing me to stay than the sea," she said.

"Good." He pulled her against him and kissed her.

Every inch of her skin inflamed. She wound her arms around his neck pressing even closer. He wore brief trunks, she a modest two-piece swimsuit. There was a lot of bare skin touching, and not for the first time Bridget wished Rashid loved her as much as she loved him. She wanted to know every inch of him. Wanted to touch him, to know her life would be complete with this wonderful man a major part of it.

His legs brushed hers as he slowly kicked to keep them upright. The contact was electric. She reveled in the exquisite sensations that pulsed through her as his kiss deepened.

A sound from the beach penetrated the haze that surrounded her and she pushed back slightly. His dark eyes looked into hers. She shivered despite the heat of the day, seeing the desire he made no effort to hide.

"Your other guests must be wondering what we are doing," she said huskily. Her breasts were pressed against his hard chest. Her legs tangled with his as he continued to keep them above the water.

"If they have eyes, they can see."

"Great." She dropped her head against his, forehead to forehead. "I think I should go in."

"You are a great one for running away," he teased.

"When in over my head, retreat is often the best strategy. At least until I can regroup."

Slowly he released her. "Regroup and come again," he said.

She swam back to the beach and came out of the water some distance from the lounge chairs. Heading for the tent, she took one of the towels a servant handed her, and wiped the water from her face before wrapping the towel around her.

Taking a soft drink offered, she stood in the edge of the shade, watching as Rashid swam parallel to the shore. His strong arms cut cleanly through the water. He was a powerful swimmer.

And powerful kisser, she thought, still feeling her heart pound.

She looked around. Mo was playing some distance away, near the water's edge with Alaya. They were constructing a huge sand castle. He was more intent in digging the moat, from what Bridget could see.

She headed for the lounge chairs. Jack and Marie were side by side. There were two empty chairs before the one Charles sat in. He was staring out at the sea, but something in his manner suggested his thoughts were far away.

The sand was warm beneath her feet, she walked slowly, sipping her beverage.

"...admit it makes sense. I always thought he should have more kids," Jack said. "He could do worse. She likes his son. Is pretty enough to have nice-looking kids. And who wouldn't like the lifestyle he enjoys."

Marie was lying on her back, eyes closed as she took in the sun. "A woman wants more than to be a good mother," she murmured.

"Well, the money he has could buy Bridget whatever she wanted."

Bridget stopped walking, stunned to find herself the topic of conversation.

"Maybe money isn't all that important. Her father made money from those restaurants. She probably has all she wants," Marie said lazily.

"Nothing like Rashid could provide," Jack countered. "I bet he proposes before we leave. She fits in. She's always in his company. They must find something to talk about."

"You don't think he's in love with her, do you?" Marie asked.

"Not that I can tell. But he's attracted to her and that would be enough."

Bridget knew it didn't pay to eavesdrop, but she was struck by the desire to hear more.

"Is that enough for you?" Marie asked.

"I don't have a kid who needs a mother."

"Mo's doing fine without one."

"No, every kid needs a mother. Want to take my bet?" Jack asked.

"You're on. I say Rashid won't propose before she leaves."

"And if he does?"

"Then I'll cook dinner for a month."

Jack was silent for a moment. Bridget was afraid to move for fear they would detect her. Could she back away without their knowing she'd overheard?

"Actually, I want something different for a bet," he said.

Marie turned and looked at him. "Like what?"

"Not dinner. I'm hoping you'll do that anyway—as my wife."

Marie sat up, her eyes only on Jack. He looked uncertain, but had his gaze on the woman at his side.

Slowly Bridget backed away until she turned and fled to the tent. It would never do to let them know she overheard their conversation.

Shocked at the thought Jack and Marie thought Rashid would propose to acquire a mother for Mo, she wanted to do nothing more than leave. She had vowed never to be second best to a man. She would not repeat the mistake her mother had made.

If she could leave this instant she would do so. Did Rashid think she was angling for marriage? That she was playing hard to get and would capitulate in the end? Was that his goal, to find a suitable mother for his son?

Charles entered the tent and went to one of the stewards. ''I need to return to the villa to get my things, then go on to the airport,'' he said.

''Yes, sir. A car will take you,'' the man replied.

''Wait,'' Bridget said on impulse. ''I want to go back with you.'' She was due to leave in two days. Maybe it would be best to make the break now, leave before she further embarrassed herself. Before Rashid had a chance to push for an answer she longed to give, but knew was wrong.

Charles looked at her, as if seeing her for the first time. ''I'm leaving,'' he said. ''Elizabeth was right about me, and I need to make things right with her.''

''Can I go with you to the airport?'' She would take a chance and book her flight when she got there. If there was nothing immediately, she'd stay in a hotel in the city. Her visit was at an end.

"Tell His Excellency I was called away," she told the steward. Snatching up her cover-up, she slipped it on, slid her feet into her shoes and stuffed the rest of her things in her tote. "I'm ready," she told Charles.

When they reached the villa, Charles alighted first and turned to assist Bridget from the car.

"Wait for me, it won't take me fifteen minutes to get ready," Bridget said.

She entered the house and flew up to her room. A quick shower to get rid of the salt-water and she dressed. In less than five minutes she had packed the clothes she came with and was ready. With a last glance at the room, she hurried down the stairs and out the front door.

The driver had already put Charles's bags into the trunk of the limousine. He took Bridget's without comment. She slid in the back seat beside Charles.

"It's rude to leave without saying good-bye," he said.

"Did you?"

He shook his head.

"Guess we'll both be chalked up as rude," she said, wishing the visit had ended differently.

Bridget looked back as they drove away, committing the house to memory. For a moment she felt a pang so sharp she had to rub her chest. She'd write to Mo, and Madame Al Besoud and Rashid. She'd come up with some excuse that she hoped would placate them. But she wouldn't come again.

Bridget settled back when they turned onto the main road. Her life would never be the same for having known Rashid.

"What do you mean, she's gone?" Rashid asked.

The maid cringed. "I checked her room. There are some clothes hanging up, but everything Miss arrived with is gone, and the suitcase, her purse, her toiletries. All gone."

He paced to the far end of the room. It was midafternoon. He hadn't seen Bridget since she had so suddenly left the beach. Once lunch with Jack and Marie had ended, he'd returned home to look for her. When he asked one of the maids to see if she was all right, he learned she'd left. With Charles? It had to be. No other car had departed today, he would have known it.

He dismissed the maid and called to the garage. The driver confirmed he'd taken two guests to the airport that morning.

She'd left. Without a word of explanation. Without a word of goodbye.

He hung up the phone, staring off into space. He clenched a fist. He had wanted her to stay longer, not leave earlier.

He'd handled the situation badly.

He went to her room. Opening the door, he stood there for several minutes, as if expecting her to rise from the chair near the window, or come from the wardrobe. The room was neatly cleaned. He crossed to the old wardrobe and opened it. He recognized some of the clothes, were they all the new ones? She hadn't taken a thing he'd paid for. A slow admiration simmered. She had been horrified when she'd discovered he had provided the clothes. This was obviously her way to mitigate the situation as far as was in her power.

He had other guests to see to. Bridget had chosen her path. He would have had it different, but so be it.

Slowly he left the room, closing the door be hind him.

CHAPTER TWELVE

IT HAD been a month since Bridget returned home. Her friends had rallied round to help her go through her father's things and to ease the transition back to normal life. His suits, dress shirts and silk ties had been donated to New Chance, the place that provided quality clothing to people to have on interviews when seeking a new chance in life after circumstances had beaten them down. The rest she donated to a homeless shelter.

Antonio had taken some mementoes he especially wanted from their papa. And offered her a job at the restaurant. She'd turned it down, resuming her duties at the library.

She was at the family home now, trying to decide if she wanted to rent it out, or move back. Nothing felt right.

Upon her return to San Francisco, she'd written to Rashid, enclosing a note also for

Madame and Mo. Not having his address, however, she'd merely sent it to the capital city, having no way of knowing if it reached him or not. Surely he was known throughout Aboul Sari.

Despite her firm hope, her love for Rashid hadn't faded once she took off from Alidan. Given time, she was sure it would. At least she hoped it would.

Funny, she'd longed for love for so long, and when it came, she had to turn her back and leave it behind. Life wasn't always fair, as her mother had probably known.

Time would heal all aches. She wished it would hurry up. She found herself gazing off into space at the most inopportune times— like now when she should finish the vacuuming of the living room. She remembered telling Mo and Rashid she did all the work in her home. She also remembered the special way Rashid would turn his head and look at her, or the passion of his kisses, or the startled laughter when his friends said something funny.

Someday she'd stop thinking every dark-haired man she saw was Rashid. Like the man climbing the stairs to the house, she thought, her daydreams fading as she focused.

Looking beyond him she saw the black limousine, and a familiar bodyguard standing at the foot of the stairs, a suitcase at his feet.

Good grief, it *was* Rashid!

Bridget hurried to the door before he could knock. She flung it open, stunned to see him.

"Hello, Bridget," he said.

"Rashid. What brings you here?"

"I would have called ahead, but felt you might refuse to see me. I must have offended you a great deal for you to leave so abruptly."

"No, you didn't offend me at all. I left for another reason. A bunch of reasons, actually."

He snapped his fingers and the bodyguard lifted the suitcase, climbing up the stairs and depositing it at Bridget's feet.

"You forgot a few things," Rashid said.

She looked at the suitcase. Her clothes, she knew. "I didn't think I should take them."

"They are yours. If I have to accept payment for them so you will take them, I will do so. But they didn't cost much and it would give me pleasure for you to have them."

"Thank you." She bit her lip. What she really wanted to know was what he was doing here. He hadn't come all the way from Aboul Sari to deliver her dresses. He could have sent them for that matter. Or given them away.

"Are you going to invite me inside?" he asked.

"Oh, yes, of course. Come in. Do your men want to come in as well?"

"No, they're fine."

"In the chilly fog?" The gray mist blew in from the ocean, obscuring the sun, giving a damp chill to the air.

"It's a nice contrast from the heat of Aboul Sari."

When he stepped into the living room, Bridget followed, flustered to see the vacuum cleaner in the center of the room.

He didn't notice.

But he did seem to fill the spacious room, taking what air there was out of it. Or was it only her starved senses, taking in every inch of him? She didn't know why he was here, but she was glad he'd come to see her. Oh, how she wished things had been different.

"Did you get my letter?" she asked.

"Yes. As did my grandmother and Mo. They miss you. It was...unfortunate...you neglected to bid them farewell when you left."

"Yes, I'm sorry. That was rude. Charles pointed that out. Of course I knew that, but I just had to go. I...just had to."

"Apparently."

She looked at him. No, he hadn't a clue. And she'd make darn sure it stayed that way.

"Have a seat. Do you want anything to drink? Coffee?" she asked.

"No. Come sit beside me."

She hesitated. "Why are you here, Rashid?"

He sat on the sofa and stretched out his long legs, studying the tips of his polished shoes. "Mo was very disappointed to discover you had left so suddenly."

She crossed the room to sit gingerly beside him on the sofa, leaving a healthy buffer space.

"I sent him a note in the letter to you."

"What precipitated your flight? The kiss in the sea? The invitation to stay?"

Bridget went still, felt the heat rise in her throat and cheeks. She dare not tell him the real reason.

He studied her for a moment, his dark eyes giving nothing away. "Jack and Marie suggested there was something between you and me."

Bridget cleared her throat nervously. "Something between us?"

He reached out his hand. Bridget stared at it for a long moment, then slowly raised hers as if compelled. When he tightened his fingers around hers, she felt her heart skip a beat.

"I know you think I'm the kind of man who would accept his parents' ideal of a woman, and never choose one for himself. I am not. I married to please them when I was younger. I grew to love Fatima from the moment we became betrothed and loved her until she died. I would not dishonor my future wife by not loving her in the same way."

She widened her eyes. "What do you mean?"

For one wild, crazy second Bridget almost thought Rashid was nervous. She stifled a giggle. The man had never had a nervous moment in his life.

Then he surprised her. "Will you marry me, Bridget Rossi? Become my wife. I pledge total fidelity as long as we both live."

He wanted to marry her? He saw her as a suitable wife? Then the conversation overheard at the beach echoed.

"I appreciate your offer but—"

"This time I'm not going for my parents' choice, but mine."

She was getting confused. His holding her hand didn't help, it scrambled her brains because all she could think of was how much she wanted him to pull her into his arms and kiss her. If he really wanted to marry her, wouldn't he want to kiss her?

''Your parents would probably not find me suitable,'' she said, trying to think.

''I think you are perfectly suitable. But that's not the overwhelming criteria for this marriage,'' he said.

''It isn't? What is?'' Her heart drummed so strongly in her chest she wondered if he could see it. Blood rushed through her veins.

''Love.''

She stared at him. Now she knew she wasn't hearing him correctly.

''Love? I thought you loved Fatima,'' she said stupidly.

''I did. That changed the day you left.''

''I left and you stopped loving Fatima?''

''You left and I was lost. I found myself unable to work because I was worried about you. Unable to sleep at night without dreaming of you. Unable to enjoy my new relationship with my son, without thinking of how you brought it about, and how everything we did was that much more fun when you were there.''

''Rashid—''

''You left and I realized you'd taken my heart with you. This past month has been hell. I'm astonished to suddenly discover love that is so overpowering I can't function because of it. That I long for a woman that I met only weeks ago, and I don't even know if she likes me, or can ever return my feelings. I've come to wine and dine you, strew roses at your feet and do all I can to make a romantic proposal. I want you for my wife.''

''Oh, Rashid!'' She flung her arms around his neck. His kiss swept away any trace of doubt as he hugged her tightly to him, his mouth claiming hers forever.

When they came up for air, he rested his forehead on hers. ''So is that a yes?''

''Yes, a thousand times, yes! I love you! I don't need to be wined or dined, or have roses strewn at my feet, but it might be nice, if you really want to.''

''I love you.'' He kissed her again. ''I'll order five dozen roses today. How soon will you become my wife?''

''As soon as it can be arranged. I can't believe this.'' She looked at him suspiciously. ''You're sure you love me? Remember I told you my father loved his first wife all his life, even though he was married to my mother and they had more than twenty years together.''

''I am not your father. I loved Fatima. But she is gone these three years. I love you differently, more than I ever thought possible. Tell me again you love me,'' he ordered.

She smiled as she looked into his eyes. ''I'll probably tell you a hundred times a day. I love you. I have loved you since that day you so kindly invited me to visit to help me deal with Papa's death, I think. You were so kind. No one in my family seemed to understand, but you did. Spending time with you in Aboul Sari only strengthened my feeling until I felt as if I were ripping out my heart when I left.''

''And for nought, except to have me come after you. When I apply your thirty-year scenario, I can't imagine being with anyone but you.''

Bridget snuggled closer, relishing every word.

She looked around the living room of her childhood home. ''I guess I'll be selling this place after all.''

''Only if you wish. Or you could save it for one of our children, maybe they'd like to live in San Francisco.''

She looked up at him and smiled. ''One of our children?''

''You said you wanted a half dozen. If they all turn out as delightful as Mo, we'll fill our lives with happiness.''

''Being with you will fill my life with happiness, but I would like to have a houseful of babies. Your babies,'' she said.

''The villa is large, we can have as many as you like.'' He brought her hand to his mouth, kissing the palm, holding it against his heart. "And your leaving convinced me my life would be devoid of all that makes it worth living without you there. I love you, Bridget. Come share your life with me."

One Year Later

Francesca leaned over the crib, studying the little girl who snuggled so serenely in her soft white blanket.

"So you found the love of your life," she said to Bridget, meeting her cousin's eyes across the crib.

"Yes. I'm so happy. Do you feel like a fairy godmother, introducing us?"

"A role I never suspected," Francesca said, trailing a finger gently down one rounded, rosy baby cheek. "He made his own choice, once he met you. I know you still miss Uncle Paolo, but look what came out of that sad time."

Bridget laughed. "Aboul Sari is much closer to Italy than San Francisco is. Come visit more often."

"I'll stay until your happiness drives me away. But I will come more often. Love becomes you both. Thank you for extending it to me."

"You're my dearest cousin. We want to share it with you," Bridget said.

Rashid stood in the doorway. Bridget smiled over at him.

"You're right, Francesca, love becomes us both," he said.

The look in his eyes still set her heart racing. Bridget expected it always would.

MILLS & BOON® PUBLISH EIGHT LARGE PRINT TITLES A MONTH. THESE ARE THE EIGHT TITLES FOR MAY 2005

————— ❦ —————

HE GREEK TYCOON'S CONVENIENT MISTRESS
Lynne Graham

HIS MARRIAGE ULTIMATUM
Helen Brooks

THE SHEIKH'S CONVENIENT BRIDE
Sandra Marton

THE MARCHESE'S LOVE-CHILD
Sara Craven

ASSIGNMENT: TWINS
Leigh Michaels

HER DESERT FAMILY
Barbara McMahon

HOW TO MARRY A BILLIONAIRE
Ally Blake

HER REAL-LIFE HERO
Trish Wylie

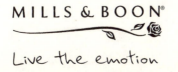

MILLS & BOON®

Live the emotion

0405 Rom LP

MILLS & BOON® PUBLISH EIGHT LARGE PRINT TITLES A MONTH. THESE ARE THE EIGHT TITLES FOR JUNE 2005

———————— ❦ ————————

HIS BOUGHT MISTRESS
Emma Darcy

BEDDED BY BLACKMAIL
Julia James

THE PRINCE'S LOVE-CHILD
Sharon Kendrick

IN THE SHEIKH'S MARRIAGE BED
Sarah Morgan

TO MARRY FOR DUTY
Rebecca Winters

HER WISH-LIST BRIDEGROOM
Liz Fielding

THE FIANCÉE CHARADE
Darcy Maguire

HER UNEXPECTED BABY
Trish Wylie

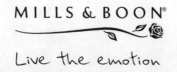

MILLS & BOON®

Live the emotion

0505 R